I0739862

His *Name* is the *Word of God*

Adam LiVecchi

Acknowledgements

Special thanks for help with the book - My beautiful and beloved Sarah, Rev. Mac Barnes and Jeanine Giuffrida.

Special thanks to my father, mother and brother Aaron. I call you guys "the family." Thanks for believing in me and encouraging me to pursue God's dreams for my life.

Special thanks to friends in ministry:

John Natale
www.johnnatale.net

Abner Suarez
www.abnersuarez.com

Mac Barnes
www.haiticharity.org

Steve & Christina Stewart
www.impactnations.com

Some other ministry friends to check out:

Jonathan Welton
www.jonwelton.com

Nic & Rachel Billman
www.shoresofgrace.com

Contents

A tribute to the best Teacher, Holy Spirit...

You are The Spirit of Truth, The Spirit of Life, The Spirit of Holiness, The Spirit of Burning and Judgment, The Spirit of Adoption, The Spirit of Grace and Supplications, The Spirit of Intercession, The Spirit of Prophesy, The Eternal Spirit, The Spirit of Wisdom and Revelation, The Spirit of Counsel and Might, The Spirit of Knowledge and of the Fear of the Lord, The Spirit of Wisdom and Understanding, The Spirit of the Living God, The Spirit of Glory. The Spirit that raised Jesus from the dead. The Spirit that JESUS gave up from the cross, the Spirit that was poured out in Acts 2. He is the Comforter. The Spirit that lead Jesus into the wilderness, The Spirit that came upon Jesus in Bodily form at the river Jordan. The Spirit that searches the deep things of God. You are the seal of our salvation. You are the seven lamps that burn before the throne of God that illuminate and make the rainbow over the throne; You lead us into all Truth!

Always tells the truth, never calls in sick, you don't have to pay Him money, He comes by personal invitation and divine orchestration. He doesn't take out His anger on you if He's grieved with someone else. He's not religious! Any time you want to be taught He'll teach. The more time you spend with Him the stronger you become. He loves His job. He doesn't just do it for a paycheck. He doesn't greet you with a weird hug if you're from another church. If you don't speak His language He'll teach you. If you don't speak His language He'll speak yours, He's so humble.

He baptizes the Word and brings light and presents Jesus, He reminds us of what Jesus said. He gets the highest recommendations from Jesus! He doesn't operate in the spirit of confusion, there's nothing He doesn't understand. His teaching is applicable for today; He doesn't throw things in your face and say I told you so, He picks you up.

He's always loving, patient, kind, truthful, merciful, and righteous all at the same time. He doesn't ask you to do a whole bunch of stuff and then not be satisfied anyway. He teaches those who others won't. He doesn't get jealous if you go to another church where there's more of Him! He never lies about being sick for a golf day. He brings revelation from the Father, not information from the wisdom of man. He doesn't answer to a religious system that wants to control you in the name of order!

He wants to empower you, give you gifts and send you! He wants to bring fruit to your tree so men can know who has bought you with His precious blood. He will convict and comfort you all in one breath. When He comes into the room everything changes.

Holy Spirit can be loud or quiet a mighty rushing wind or a still small voice, He always does the Father's will! He does what's best for you, even if it hurts. He's never to busy, there's no material He's unfamiliar with, and He never forgets anyone's name. He's no respecter of persons, He doesn't have affairs with students, and He will help during a test.

He doesn't get sick of your questions if you're serious. He raises the dead. He leads by example, not theory or a theological idea. He doesn't teach false doctrine to fi t His lack of faith. He doesn't teach things to manipulate you for His personal gain; He loves Jesus with all of His heart. He's in perfect relation with the Father and the Son. He never displeased the Father or the Son, He's never failed anyone. Holy Spirit is never boring to listen to. He's never stagnant, He's always on the move, He never smells bad, He wears the fragrance of Christ, for He is the Spirit of Jesus Christ.

Evil spirits are subject to Him. Man pleasers can't please Him, you can never have too much of Him, He doesn't leave unless you push Him away; challenge is not a word in His vocabulary, Victory is.

He doesn't need a power point, He is power…He understands Greek and Hebrew, He doesn't use verses out of context. He is the excellent Spirit that was in Daniel. If you ever want to see what He's teaching you, He will show you. He goes on field trips; He should be the Head of every mission's board in every Church. He blows you away, His fi re cleans our mouths. In His class one person can be laughing and one person crying, and there is no confusion. His classes offend the religious and draw the hungry and thirsty! He knows how to pronounce all those big Old Testament names in the genealogies. He hears everything you say behind His back, He hears when you talk bad about the Lamb's wife, and He's grieved! No one can stop Him from being who He is. He's not insecure, He's never worried, He has no Fear, and He has no lack. He is the Breath of Life; He is God!

Please don't quench Him, please don't grieve Him, He is God's gift to us, speak to Him, and ask Him questions; give Him your prayer requests. Let Him speak to you and lead you.

Holy Spirit we love and honor You!

"And all that dwell upon the earth shall worship him, whose names are not written in the book of life of the Lamb slain from before the foundation of the world" (Revelation 13:8).

First understand that the "him" that is worshipped in this verse is not Jesus, the Lamb, but the beast or the antichrist (2 *Thessalonians 2:3*). The demise of worshipping such a hideous creature is for those whose "names are not written in the book of life." Yet the beast is not the focus of this book. The most intriguing idea in Revelation 13:8 is that the Lamb was slain from before the foundation of the world. One can also believe that it is also very probable that His book, the Lamb's Book of Life, was also written before the foundation of the world. Just think on that for a few minutes. God, Yahweh, is an all knowing and unchanging God. He knew who would accept Him and who would not. That is why in Jesus' earthly ministry He said, narrow is the way that leads to life and few find it.

The last move of God in the earth will be a corporate understanding of whom we, the church, will marry a slain lamb. The church will grow in bridal love as the revelation of Jesus as a slain lamb comes back to the forefront of the church. When we receive our new bodies in heaven, Jesus who never changes, will still bear our proof of purchase in His body. He will still have holes in His feet and hands, and a wound on His side. I fully believe that the only possible way to overcome, to not love our life and to resist the end time apostasy of the church (that is here right now) is to receive a Revelation of the Lamb. The last book of the Bible, which came from the Lamb's "book," is the revelation of Jesus Christ. Jesus says, "My words are Spirit and life." The last book of the Bible is all about the Lamb being revealed for all that He is. The first four chapters of Revelation do not mention Him as a Lamb. In chapter five, Jesus is revealed as a slain Lamb. After that, the primary name used for Jesus is, "the Lamb;" He was revealed wounded, full of wrath, so much so that men hide from Him. All these words are Spirit and Life, so the last outpouring will be a Revelation of the Lamb who is Worthy, and there will be a wave of Martyrdom. There will be a company of people who's blood speaks, "worthy is the Lamb that was slain."

John the Revelator, who is the Author of the book of Revelation, was in the Spirit. Rather, he was poured into the Spirit, not only the Spirit on him and then in him but he was drowned in the Spirit on the Lord's Day when this whole book of Revelation began. John was on the island of Patmos for the Word of God and the testimony of Jesus. He was faithful to preach what he knew, and God was faithful to reveal more to him. He was submersed or drowned in God's river, and he received the Revelation of the Lamb. Some revelation comes while we are still alive to the flesh. For example, in Matthew 16, Peter said to Jesus, *"you are the Christ;"* then in only a few verses later Jesus is telling Peter, *"Get behind me Satan."* Peter's flesh was a dominant reality in his life. However, when John received the visions that made up the book of Revelation, he truly was crucified with Christ, so much so that the Father revealed Jesus to him as a slain Lamb. Remember, John stood at Jesus' cross during Jesus' crucifixion. Now the Father desired John to go deeper into who

Jesus is. This revelation would end the Bible itself. John saw Jesus' life come to an end, and he had the privilege of putting the finishing touches on the Bible and seeing the canon of scripture come to an end also. I briefly mentioned Peter because the revelation that Jesus was the Son of God was supposed to help Peter understand Jesus' sacrifice as a part of God's plan. When Peter received this revelation it didn't change his perception or understanding of God's purposes in Christ. We receive revelation so that we change how we see, which helps us change how we live and view life.

Jesus' side was pierced while He was on the cross, but after He had offered up His Spirit. Our piercing comes after we meet Jesus on the cross and offer our will to God in exchange for His. When we offer our will to God, His word comes to us in a more clear fashion, as it mentions in Revelation 3:19. When we surrender our will, we are positioning ourselves for God's will which is defined clearly in His word. The revelation that came to John came while he was in exile for preaching the Word of God and the testimony of Jesus. The revelation also came after John's will was fully surrendered. The revelation of the Lamb will come to those who have surrendered hearts and want more of God. The piercing that happened to Mary, at the foot of the cross of Jesus, will happen to a generation of wise virgins. Wise virgins are those who sit at the feet of Jesus and cultivate a hearing ear and a burning heart. A hearing ear and a burning heart will lead to a lifestyle of obedience to God's word and outpourings of His Spirit.

With the truth that the Lamb was slain from before the foundation of the world, let us now approach creation. Both Paul and John agree that Jesus, or the Word of God, created all things. We see these scriptures both point directly to Jesus as Creator (John 1:1-3, and Colossians 1:16, 1:20).

Paul takes it somewhere interesting, let's read these two verses in Colossians:

"For by Him were all things created, that are in heaven, and that are in the earth, visible and invisible, whether thrones, or dominions, or principalities, or powers: all things were created by Him, and for Him" (Colossians 1:16).

"And having made peace through the blood of His cross, by Him to reconcile all things unto Himself; by Him, I say, whether they be things in the earth, or things in the heaven" (Colossians 1:20).

Paul speaks about creation and redemption; is it possible that the Creator, during creation, had redemption on His mind, because He was the Lamb slain from before the foundation of the world? At creation, did Jesus the Word of God have the cross on His mind when He was creating?

I have some interesting thoughts to present to you about creation. Consider this, if the Lamb was slain from before the foundation of the world, and the Lamb wrote the Book of Life, and Abel offered a Lamb before the law told him he had to; then perhaps while Jesus was creating the world, the cross was on His mind. Let's look at our Creator's order in which He created.

First, before God ever speaks, according to the scripture, the Spirit of God was moving upon the face of the deep. So before God even spoke, the Spirit of the Lord was already waiting to fulfill what was spoken. The Spirit of God was positioned to fulfill the Word before it was even spoken. (see Genesis 1:1-2) Then God speaks and says, "Let there be light" and there was light. This is not sunlight; this is "Son" light. Later in Genesis 1:14, we see the division of day from night, the light from the dark. Yet in Jesus there is no darkness, a kingdom divided cannot stand, in Jesus there is only light. So now we know that Jesus is the Light of the World. Jesus who is the Lamb slain from before the foundation of the world, is the Creator, He is the Word that was with God, the Word that was God and the Word that will always be God. Jesus Christ, according to the scripture, is the same yesterday, today and forever. Jesus is the Lamb slain from before the foundation of the world, so it would make sense to have the cross on His mind if He were already the slain Lamb.

On day three of creation the slain Creator, who has the cross in His mind, creates vegetation as explained in the following verse. *"And the earth brought forth grass, and herb yielding seed after his kind, and tree yielding fruit whose seed was in itself, after his kind: and God saw it was good"* (Genesis 1:12). Seed has to go into the ground and die before it can bear fruit. This is a picture of death and resurrection; this is a picture of being crucified with Christ and then having the fruit of His Spirit, the very evidence of His existence, in you. The Creator on the third day of creation, created a seed. That seed bears life in it, but that life is only edible for others after it has died. Sunlight and water have nurtured it and then fruit becomes visible and evident, then ripe and edible. The harvest is not only a soul being saved, yet it is fruit being ripe. We become the harvest by baring spiritual fruit, as in love, peace, and joy (see Galatians 5:22-23). It is very important that we are the harvest before we become laborers in Jesus' harvest. Then in the very same verse (Genesis 1:12) we have a tree yielding fruit with its seed in itself. The only way to produce fruit is to be an extension or a branch on the True Vine, being Jesus Christ. In creation we have the slain Redeemer creating a tree with its seed in itself, and also a seed that's fruit bearing. These are both being simultaneously created as Jesus opens His mouth and speaks. Jesus is creating a fruit bearing seed on the third day, knowing He is the "corn of wheat" that will die and rise according to the word He will inspire Isaiah to speak. Jesus knows everything, and so He knew that on the third day when He created a tree, He would rise on the third day from being crucified on a tree. There are no coincidences with an all-knowing, Almighty God. Jesus was fully aware that He was that seed that produces after His kind. Through Jesus offering His divine Spirit, the Spirit of God from the cross, we become partakers of His divine nature. The same Spirit that raised Him from the dead lives in us and continuously puts an end to our old life, our old views, our feelings, and ways of thinking. We begin to bear the fruit that is only possible if you have been grafted into the Tree of Life. Not only are the cross and the resurrection on His mind, but literally the consummation of all things unto His headship. The purpose of the cross and the resurrection is for the consummation of all things unto His headship, or sovereign and eternal leadership. Jesus Christ, the God man, was manifesting the wisdom of God even before the first man and the whole world was done being created.

Then after this we see on the fourth day of creation, light at Jesus' word to divide the day from the night. His word does not divide soul and spirit, but it divides light from dark. So here His word defines time and seasons. That is really interesting because Jesus' death splits time itself in half. There is usually division when God speaks. *"There was a division again among the Jews for these sayings"* (John 10:19). Here is another example; *"Father, glorify thy name. Then there came a voice from heaven, saying, I have both glorified it, and will glorify it again. Then the people therefore stood by and hear it, said, that it thundered: others said, an angel spoke to him"* (John 12:28-29). Jesus responds by saying that the voice came not because of Me, but for you. Both groups were wrong. They were divided with their wrong perceptions of God's voice.

Day six of creation, the slain Creator created man in His image; Jesus was crucified on His creation, meaning a tree, by His creation, meaning humans, and for His creation, meaning you and me. He hung on the cross for six hours and He created man on the sixth day. He redeemed man by becoming sin, hanging there for six hours, offering up His Divine Spirit. His rising three days later translated us out of Adam and out of the sixth day, the number of man, which grafted us into a company of the third day, a company of resurrected son's and daughters of the King Himself. There is no way I could have seen this on my own, and there is nothing we can discover outside of an all-knowing, omnipresent God who chose in His wisdom to take up residence on the inside of us. It fascinates me how much the cross was on His mind to see that He would create a tree with its seed inside itself, knowing He's the tree and I am the seed. If He knew us before the world began, than possibly He knew who would accept Him and who would not. Predestination is not Jesus choosing for us, but knowing our choices before we make them. If we were in Him before the world began, and the Lamb's book was written before the Law the Prophets or the New Testament, perhaps He knew everything that was going to happen before it happened. Perhaps He sees the end from the beginning. He is the Alpha and the Omega, the Beginning and the Ending, the Almighty, the First and the Last. It is very important to see that scripture is all about Jesus, that God is good, and to begin to understand God's heart towards you, so you can have His heart for others.

It saddens me to say that the Bible is probably the most misunderstood and miss-appropriated book ever. Even currently, it is the best selling book, it still has produced the most blood shed through the ages because it is God's word. The Bible is infallible, but its readers are not. Due to this, Jesus has become the most misrepresented, and misunderstood person ever to walk the face of the earth. If we allow Jesus to lead us and not our flesh, we will be enlightened to truth and not lead others into deception. When we approach the Word of God it should be with fear and trembling and with the mind of Christ. In turn a resurrected Jesus will open the scriptures to us, teaching us not only His Word but also His ways. This will keep us from deception, offense, and also misrepresenting The Author of the Book.

One must understand that God knows everything about us, and was willing to be slain for us before we were even able to make mistakes or confess and repent for them. Grasping this concept is definitely the door to receiving a fascinated heart, which continually gazes upon the beauty of the Lord in His word. The depth of the sacrifice of the Lamb is also the only wineskin, or theology, that can fully understand the end times, without becoming offended. Before John the Revelator got a whole picture of the end times, 96 years after Jesus had died, he saw Him as a Lamb bearing wounds still in timeless eternity. Why would the Holy Spirit allow him to see Jesus in such a way when He was at the foot of the cross, when He acquired those wounds? The mighty Holy Spirit allowed John to see what the Father sees, then later shows him what the Father's doing in the times to come. Seeing what the Father is doing without seeing what the Father sees, could cause a problem that the Holy Spirit did not want to put John through. John was already in exile for the testimony of Jesus and the Word of God. The word of God gives us God's perspective, which keeps us from deception and leads us to blessing called Truth who is a person.

Jesus, who is the Word of God, is absolutely good. The writer of Hebrews speaks of tasting the "Good Word of God and the powers of the age to come." Perhaps what he is referring to is the need to experience Jesus and His power. Jesus gives us life, breath, and a free will. Then makes Himself vulnerable and becomes subject to how we treat Him, and allows us to choose to accept His purchase from Calvary. How we treat the Word of God is how much we value Christ being crucified for us. When I use the word "treat," I mean do we obey what God has clearly revealed or not? Jesus said, if you love Me, you will keep My commandments or My word. Our love for Him and His presence is seen by how we keep His commandments, not by how loud we sing at church. Jesus is only our Lord if we hear His word and obey it. Jesus asks an amazing question in the book of Luke; *"Why do you call me Lord, Lord if you do not do what I say?"* He's not looking for a slick religious answer but a repentant heart that will only have room in it for His word.

When the people whom God has put in authority have no regard for the Word of the Lord, the people of God become besieged or taken captive. The authority that God had delegated to protect, becomes the very reason God's people are plundered and taken captive. Welcome to the church of today by and large. However, in the season of judgment or wilderness, the next generation is formed in affliction and conformed into the image of Christ. Let us look at how the book of Daniel came to be, as seen in Jeremiah 36. Daniel 1:1, is a fulfillment of a prophetic word released by Jeremiah. Prophets who are sent to the people of God tend to have more continual problems than Prophets who prophesy to Babylon. Daniel had one test, which was the lion's den. Daniel's resilience to not compromise God's word gave him the ability to pass the test. Daniel kept God's word and God released His power. This gave way to the good news of the Kingdom of God to go to every person in the earth. However, Jeremiah is always getting into problems; prison, a ditch full of human waste, all kinds of stuff. The covenant people of God are sometimes the hardest people to deal with. Please don't ask me how I know.

I wasn't always a Christian. I used to be a small time drug dealer and I can honestly say I had fewer problems selling drugs than ministering in churches. I am not sharing this to glorify the past or beat on the church, however, I can in one-way or another, identify with the various troubles that are attached to the Truth. Paul said, *"Am I your enemy because I tell you the truth?"* (Galatians 4:16). Paul understands Jeremiah's woes. Religion put 39 stripes on Paul's back, five times. Religion accepts the written word, but rejects God's now word.

Jeremiah 36 has an interesting story. In this passage Jeremiah has a prophetic word for King Jehoiakim, the current King of Judah. After his men read the prophecy to him, he rejected it. Jehudi cut the scroll with a penknife and threw it into the fire, until the scroll was consumed. The shame of the matter is the leadership of God's covenant people had no interest in the Word of the Lord. This is common today, but it seems to be changing for the better. I see a new hunger emerging in the people of God. Recently I had a vision of a beautiful woman, who was dressed in a bridal gown. When she opened her mouth, she was teething like a little child. The teeth were just starting to break the gum. At that moment, I heard the Spirit of the Lord say, "the bride is getting hungry." There is a company of people who fear God and tremble at His Word; those who's hearts ache to see the Holy Spirit put Jesus on display through their lives, those who want to be reminded of His words, those who are not ashamed of His words.

This disregard of God's word had drastic ramifications. Jehoiakim was a King of Judah, however, his name is not written in the lineage of Jesus. *"And if any man shall take away from the words of the book of this prophecy, God shall take away his part out of the book of life, and out of the Holy city, and from the things which are written in this book"* (Revelation 22:12). Jesus, the Word knows everything; He knew that Jehoiakim's name would not be in Jesus' lineage due to his complete disregard for it. Jehoiakim's iniquity affected him, his servants, and his seed. It also affected the people of God, who may not have been in agreement with his decision to cut the Word of the Lord up and throw it in the fire.

Jeremiah's prophetic word; *"And thou shalt say to Jehoiakim king of Judah, Thus saith the Lord; Thou hast burned this roll, saying, Why hast thou written therein, saying, The kingdom of Babylon shall certainly come and destroy this land, and shall cause to cease from thence man and beast? Therefore thus saith the Lord of Jehoiakim king of Judah; He shall have none to sit upon the throne of David: and his dead body shall be cast out in the day to the heat, and in the night to the frost. And I will punish him and his seed and his servants for their iniquity; and I will bring upon them, and upon the inhabitants of Jerusalem, and upon the men of Judah, all the evil that I have pronounced against them; but they hearkened not"* (Jeremiah 36:29-31).

This prophetic word was given 607 B.C. The word was fulfilled in the same year. It is referred to in Daniel; *"In the third year of the reign of Jehoiakim king of Judah came Nebuchadnezzar king of Babylon unto Jerusalem, and besieged it"* (Daniel 1:1). With the besieging of Jerusalem and the people of God, went some of the treasures from the house of God into the land of Shinar to the house of a false god. The people of God and the treasure of God go together, for we are the pearl that the Merchant sold all of His possessions to purchase it. Jesus came to seek and save us, although He may find us in the darkness of the earth in the depravity of our sin. The people of God are His greatest investment; this is why we should hold His Word in the highest regard. If He holds us in such high esteem, we should really value His word above anything else. It is crucial in this hour, that we understand His Word, hear His voice and obey Him. The oppression of God's people was God's judgment, because they did not hear or obey His word. Oppressive and abusive authority is one of the ways God judges His people.

What is scary to me is that the leadership of Judah cut up the scroll and threw it in the fire. This is a picture of the stripes of our Lord, and how He was thrown to the pagans to be nailed to a cross. He became our burnt offering as He was thrown into the fire willingly, by His own choice, to be consumed in the wrath of God for us. *"He answered and said, Lo, I see four men loose, walking in the midst of the fire, and they have no hurt; and the form of the forth is like the Son of God"* (Daniel 3:25). King Jehoiakim threw the Word of the Lord in the fire, the King of Babylon threw the people of God in the fire, and Jesus appeared there. When Jesus showed up, the people of God were loosed. What the enemy meant for evil, God turned to good for those who loved Him enough to stand for Him and not bow to idols. When we stand up for God, He shows up for us. When Jesus comes on the scene the bound get free, which is a great picture of the Gospel in motion. Their walk of faith got them into the furnace, and whom their faith was in, freed them in it, and protected them from it. Many want to be protected from it, but Jesus protects you in it. They were not kept from the fire, but from the ramifications of the fire. The real fascinating part is, they didn't hear from the Lord before the fire or in the fire. His Law was written in their hearts, they would keep it no matter the cost. They kept His word and He manifested Himself as He promised. *"He that hath my commandments, and keepeth them, he it is that loveth me: he that loveth me shall be loved of my Father, and I will love him and will manifest myself to him"* (John 14:21). So they kept the law and Jesus manifests Himself to them and laws change. (see Daniel 3:29- 4:3) Jesus shows up and doesn't even say a word while He was in the fire, no altar call, no sinner's prayer. He is so mighty to save that He doesn't have to speak to accomplish His will; His presence alone is enough. I am fully persuaded that this was Jesus. He appeared in human form to show that the wrath of man cannot harm Him; also that He is faithful to deliver. Jesus is the Word; therefore He doesn't have to speak to save. He alone can save men from the fire and from death. Death has no dominion over Him or His devoted followers who love not their lives unto death. The revelation of Jesus Christ is what true believers live for and from. Jehoiakim tried to get rid of Jesus' words by fire, and then Jesus appears in the fire. Nebuchadnezzar tries to make them bow, and he winds up bowing to God of the Heavens and writing a decree. *"Therefore I make a decree, that every people nation and language which speak anything amiss against the God of Shadrach, Meshach, and Abed-nego, shall be cut in pieces, and their houses shall be made a dung hill: because there is no other God who can deliver after this sort"* (Daniel 3:29).

So Jehoiakim did not want to hear the Word of the Lord, then God uses Nebuchadnezzar to tell the whole world the testimony of what God had done. First Jehoiakim cuts the Word of the Lord up and throws it into the fire, and then anyone who speaks against the God of the Word will be cut up and thrown into a dunghill.

Nebuchadnezzar tried to make them bow, and he ended up bowing to the Lord God of the Heavens. Also the second time that Jeremiah wrote the scroll, the end of the verse reads, *"and there were besides unto them many like words"* (Jeremiah 36:23). I call this the prosperity of the Word; you try to throw the Word of the Lord in the Fire, and yet the Word goes out to the whole world and Babylon pays for the shipping and handling. Here the Word of the Lord prevailed, in time and space, simply because six knees did not bow down to a false god. The Lord uses a heathen to get the good news of the Kingdom into the entire world. The Word of the Lord was cut and thrown into the fire, and then a law was established that if you speak against the God of this Word, who alone is able to deliver, you will be cut up and thrown into a dunghill, with your house also.

We are either of the company who have no regard for the Word, or of the company where the Word Himself manifests and delivers us from evil personally. Do we regard the Word of the Lord or attempt to throw Him away by disobedience, because of a hardened heart? His Word is truth and truth sets us free. We should not reject His attempt to free us. It was for freedom Christ set us free. Every time He opens His mouth to speak, it is so that we can be clean and free. Clean to be His reflection and free to walk with Him.

We get free from Egypt in order to posses a land flowing with milk and honey. God's design was to take His covenant people out of Egypt and from the House of Bondage. God doesn't just want His people out of Egypt; He wants Egypt out of His people. His desire was for His Word to be a lamp unto their feet and a light unto their path. He even wanted to deliver them from the shadow of Egypt. Meaning, the cloud or the shadow of their past is not going to determine their future if they would simply hear and obey. God's desire was for His presence and His Word to define their future. There was a cloud by day and a fire by night. They had already seen what the blood of the Lamb was capable of before they even had the Law, written by Moses. Israel was already living in the freedom that they had received by God's mighty hand and His long outstretched arm. They were familiar with the prosperity that Egypt had given them. They continuously encountered miraculous deliverance, miraculous provision, and literally being led by the presence of God. They had the humblest man on the face of the earth as their leader. This was all good but God is the God of exceedingly more than we can ask, think, or imagine. God had a lot more for them than this.

Before they were taken out from Egypt, they saw what the blood could do while they were in Egypt. The Blood of the Lamb will soon become one of the main topics of the church again, as the judgments of God are around the corner. Experiencing the light of God's word is the only cure for the shadow of Egypt. Light comes from the mouth of God, whether it be God's command or God's counsel (Genesis 1:3). As great as being led by God's presence is, as great as miraculous deliverance and provision are, God always has more good in store for His people. Before the Land of Promise was possessed, the people of God had to go through the River of Repentance, they had to cross over the Jordan. Coming out of Egypt would be like a prophetic picture of the baptism of repentance. Crossing the Jordan is like the baptism of the Spirit that empowers one for ministry. Jesus must be met on the cross; you must be crucified with Christ, before you are established in and anointed by Him for service. The Land of Promise, or the person of Jesus, is God's destination for His covenant people. There were some reasons Moses didn't get to inhabit the Land of Promise, although He met God in Glory, and God spoke to him face to face. We tend to be prone to do exactly what Moses did and rob ourselves of God's highest intentions for us. I am not attacking Moses, Jesus chose Moses to be on the Mount of Transfiguration and Moses is a mighty man of God. I am learning from his examples as Paul tells us to. Jesus' example is what to do; men's examples are usually what not to do and what God does in spite of us.

As Moses was receiving the Law, the people were making a golden calf. Moses responds in anger and throws the Ten Commandments down and breaks them. There is a parallel here with Jesus' first coming, when He comes broken and wounded, dying for us, and then rising from the dead. Moses hand writes the Ten Commandments, the second time, and the commandments go into the Ark of the Covenant or the Presence of God. This is true with the second coming of Jesus. For after He returns the second time, we will return with Him to the presence of God our Father.

Moses threw the Ten Commandments down because the people were worshipping a golden calf that his brother helped them make. God was giving the Law and the people were breaking it. Moses responds in anger, and throws the Law of God on the ground. He does the very thing he was mad at them for doing, breaking the Law. Jesus the Word always becomes mistreated, when we do not deal with our issues. Someone with un-dealt issues will generally respond to circumstances in an inappropriate way, revealing by their words or actions that there is something deeply wrong inside. The Law of God is perfect at converting the soul; the Word gets thrown on the ground when our soul is not converted. Jesus converts our soul by fulfilling the Law we have broken. The converted soul in the Old Testament is the renewed mind in the New Testament. The renewed mind simply hears God and obeys Him.

Never put down the Word, because of the actions of others, let the Word control your actions and emotions. Never let your anger control you, for *"the wrath of man worketh not the righteousness of God"* (James1:20). That verse is very visible and plain to see in the life of Moses. Jesus came because we were lawbreakers; before the Law was written or broken, the Lamb was slain. I continuously repeat the subject of the Lamb being slain because He gave Himself so we can experience Him, and be established in His highest plans for us. His highest plans are only attained as we learn downward mobility. Downward mobility is when we humble ourselves and He exalts us in due season. We serve and He brings us into places of influence. Moses had to be drawn out of the river and out of Egypt, before he could take the people of God out. We have to have Egypt taken out of us before we can effectively take others out. Many new believers make the mistake of trying to get all their friends saved, and they wind up losing their salvation in the process. We have to come out of the world and into the Kingdom if we are ever truly going to bring others to Jesus or bring Jesus to others. The wilderness is a place of transition; in transition God deals with our issues. The deeper the sanctification we go through, the purer we reflect Jesus to those around us. When we are His reflection, those who are not looking for Him find Him in us, that is Christianity.

In Numbers 20 and Exodus 17, we see Moses striking a rock to draw water. The first time, in Exodus 17:6, Moses did it God's way, he smote the rock and water gushed forth. The second time, in Numbers 20, Moses chooses to do it his way. Many times what is started in the spirit ends in the flesh. Moses receives specific directions in Numbers 20:7-11. God's command to Moses is; *"speak ye unto the rock before their eyes; and it shall give forth water to them out of the rock. And Moses lifted up his hand and with his rod he smote the rock twice: and the water came out abundantly, and their congregation drank and their beasts also."* The first time God commanded Moses to smite the rock, this time God told him to speak to it. He disobeyed God and hit the rock. Moses was frustrated with the people so he disobeyed God. Many times frustration will lead to disobedience. If we don't deal with our past, it will surely deal with us and those who we are leading. Moses' anger or negative response to others cost him his mansion in Egypt and in the Promise Land. If we don't allow Jesus to deal with our issues, we will die overlooking what God has promised because we have not died to self.

Jesus says all that are thirsty come, and drink freely of the water of life. Paul the Apostle wrote of this rock from which Israel drank from in the wilderness, and that Rock was Christ. *"And did all drink the same spiritual drink: for they drank of that spiritual Rock that followed them: and that Rock was Christ"* (1 Corinthians 10:4). Jesus is the One who gives living water, which purifies and restores our soul and makes us whole. Our soul is restored as God's voice is heard. We become whole as we learn to perceive from God's perspective. This happens as we hear His commentary on everything we are going through. We receive access into the mind of Christ as He speaks to us.

Moses hitting the stone twice is like a picture of crucifying Jesus afresh, spoken about in Hebrews. *"For it is impossible for those who were once enlightened, and have tasted of the heavenly gift, and were made partakers of the Holy Ghost, and have tasted the good word of God, and the powers of the world to come, If they shall fall away, to renew them again unto repentance; seeing they crucify to themselves the Son of God afresh, and put him to open shame"* (Hebrews 6:4-6). Those who crucify Jesus afresh bring open shame upon the One who took our shame upon Him. This is terribly dangerous. Again Jesus suffers because of other people's bad choices. We must deeply realize that our choices affect others, for better or for worse. Jesus despised the shame and for the joy set before Him, endured the cross. That only had to be done once; similar to the fact that Moses only had to strike the rock once.

Moses did not inherit the Promise Land, but he was there when God promised it to Israel in Exodus 3. Before this promise, God brought His people out of the affliction of Egypt. He declared to Moses that He is the I AM. So even before God did anything through Moses, He first revealed Himself to Moses. God loves to reveal Himself, which is why the Word became flesh and dwelt among us. So God reveals Himself to Moses in a burning bush, then tells him what He's going to do. God briefly describes whom He is going to take and the condition of where they are going. *"And I have said, I will bring you out of the affliction of Egypt unto the land of the Canaanites, and the Hittites, and the Amorites, and the Perizzites, and the Hivites, and the Jebusites, unto a land flowing with milk and honey"* (Exodus 3:17). When God heard the groaning of His people, He then remembered His promise to Abraham. Then God appeared to Moses and commissioned him to become the solution to their problem. The full solution was the Land of Promise or the Promise Land. To fully inhabit this land, the way God intended, they would have to be free from Egypt. They also would need to have victory over their enemies, who currently inhabited the land that was promised to them. We do not obtain God's promise without confronting the enemy. Moses died before he went into the promise land even when God said, "I will bring you up out of Egypt and unto the land flowing with milk and honey." God is not a liar or a false prophet, Moses' action of smiting the rock a second time is the reason he could not inhabit the land that flows with milk and honey. If we crucify Jesus afresh, we will not inherit God's promises for our life or the Kingdom of God in the life to come. God's desire was for Israel to taste the goodness of God. The operation of the Holy Spirit in Hebrews 6 is so we would taste of the heavenly gift, which is the Holy Spirit. Paul said we "were made to drink of one Spirit." God wants us to taste the powers of the world to come, and also taste the good Word of God. God serves us a meal and then gives us a drink; He is truly better than we think. The good Word of God is a living person, whose name is the Word of God. When the Father opens His mouth to speak, it's Jesus that comes forth.

The Word of God brings a tension with it. For example, the Word is referred to as washing water, but the Word is also like a fire and fire burns. Both the water and the fire are agents of purification, depending on how dirty the object is that is in need of cleansing. During this time, God's intention was not for the Word to bring tension but blessing, due to where Israel had been for the previous 400 years. The milk of the Word was for them to be nurtured in the Word and ways of God. They had to unlearn all that they had learned in oppression. Milk is what nurtures a baby in the natural and in the spirit also. *"As newborn babes, desire (or crave long after) the sincere milk of the word, that ye may grow thereby: If so be ye tasted that the Lord is gracious (or kind)"* (1 Peter 2:2-3). God establishes His people in the sincere milk of the Word, which allows them to taste that He is good. The Promise Land was full of the goodness of God, abounding in prosperity. The highest form of prosperity is the prosperity of the Word. Paul said it like this, "Let the word of Christ dwell in you richly in all wisdom." Part of Christ's unsearchable riches is His Word. God longed to establish His people in the milk and honey of the Word. The most fundamental revelation of God is that He is good. His intention was to deeply establish that with His chosen people. They wouldn't have been chosen if He wasn't good. Water sustains and cleanses, and honey is sweet. After the bitterness of Egypt, He deeply wanted to reveal His goodness.

Psalm 81 speaks about six things God would have done "if" Israel had obeyed. Many times we limit God's doings in our life, by not doing what He has already told us to do. *"He should have fed them also with the finest of the wheat: and with honey out of the rock should I have satisfied"* (Psalm 81:16). God intends to supernaturally sustain His people by His word. Jesus said, "man does not live by bread alone, but by every word that proceeds out of the mouth of God." We live by what is proceeding out of God's mouth; the same way faith comes by hearing, not having heard. When our affections are truly set above, we are attentive to God's voice and obedient to His commands. Jesus alone satisfies. What is awesome about that Rock, who is Christ Jesus, is that water and honey flow from the same Rock. The Word of God cleanses and satisfies. The water of the Word cleanses, washes, and sustains. It waters the seed of itself; the same way the Word watches over itself to perform it. The sincere, unadulterated milk and honey of the Word are what God had in store for His people who just came out of bondage. God was leading His people to the place of experiencing and tasting the Word in the land of promise. Milk is what gets us ready for the meat of the Word; meat is for those who are of full age, those who discern evil from good. God establishes us in the goodness of who He is, so by learning to recognize and discern Him, we learn who and what is not from or of Him.

The Truth is a person and a spirit. There is one Truth, who is Jesus, who sent His Spirit to live in us. Many people have enough truth on their statement of faith to believe that they are not deceived. The only way the truth makes you free is when you know Him. A good profession means nothing if the lifestyle is not in agreement with it. To know or study all the lies is foolish, because you become full of lies. To know the Truth will allow you to identify the lies, and release light in the darkness.

"How sweet are thy words unto my taste! Yea, sweeter than honey to my mouth! Through thy precepts I get understanding: therefore I hate every false way" (Psalm 119:103-104). The sweetness of God's goodness causes the Psalmist not only to identify the false way, but also to hate it. The simplicity that God is good is very important to understand, especially in a world with lots of bad stuff happening. The goodness of God is essential to establish a believer, because when bad things happen they will not be offended. If we have really experienced the goodness of God, it's pretty hard to get offended at God even in hard times. When we try to explain what we don't understand, we only confuse people. When bad stuff happens and we don't know why, we should not pull a reason out of nowhere. We should just stop and remember that God is good, and press forward into His promises that are yes and amen in Christ. Many people try to explain the past instead of just moving onto the future by enjoying the present.

When the experience of God's word deeply becomes our experiential reality, we love what God loves and hate what He hates. This is one of the ways the Father conforms us to the image of Christ. We experience His word and we become like the One who is speaking to us, as we become like Him we feel what He feels, and see what He sees. If we keep paying attention we will say what He is saying and go where He is going. That is true ministry.

The Word is a person; He became flesh and dwelt among us. There is a tension that only Jesus brings. The day of the Lord is both great and terrible. That is an example of when Jesus shows up, there are two different realities depending on the relationship we have or do not have with Him. There is a tension that even the attributes of God create, for example, He is a God of wrath but He is also love. God is also radically merciful, or you wouldn't be reading, and I wouldn't be writing. God is also completely just. Therefore, Jesus had to be punished for us if we were going to be reinstated back into a relationship with the Father. So in the middle of the wrath of God and the mercy of God, the fear of the Lord is released causing us to live godly in Christ Jesus. This tension is what causes us to fear the Lord and to depart from evil. It is the same tension that causes us to hate sin but to love sinners as Jesus did. This beautiful tension causes us to depart from evil, but pursue sinners with the Good News of the Gospel.

Here is a brief example of this tension in the person of Jesus; the tension is seen in one of His names and what He will do. Scripture says that Jesus is the *"Prince of Peace"* in Isaiah 9:6. The same Bible says, *"The Lord is a man of war"* (Exodus 15:3). The Prince of Peace in righteousness makes war. Righteousness causes men to be persecuted as it did Paul and Peter, and even you and I. In righteousness the Prince of Peace shall make war, similar to the *"God of Peace who will crush Satan under your feet shortly"* (Romans 16:20). The word of God and the person of Jesus are the most controversial issues ever. Jesus Himself lived in this tension in a perfect way, as being fully man and fully God, while He walked this earth and even while He was walking on water.

This is seen in the Book of Revelation, the angel makes known this tension to John before he eats the book. *"And I went unto the angel, and said unto him, give me the little book. And he said unto me, Take it, and eat it up; and it shall make thy belly bitter, but it shall be in thy mouth sweet as honey. And I took the little book out of the angel's hand, and ate it up; and it was in my mouth sweet as honey: and as soon as I had eaten it, my belly was bitter"* (Revelation 10:9-10). This is also an interesting encounter. An angel is standing upon the sea and the earth when John approaches him for this little book, a voice tells him to eat, so John obeys. It was as the angel said, "sweet in his mouth and bitter to his belly." This, to me, is profound and highly interesting. It goes from tasty to bitter, after going down a few pipes and tubes and into his belly. This is fascinating how the great contrast occurs so quickly with the tension of taste.

The Word of God creates so much tension, it's beautiful. The tension is not to create confusion, but submission. For example, we are saved by grace through faith yet faith without works is dead and cannot save anyone. Without faith it is impossible to please God. Without hearing from God we cannot ever have the faith to please Him. Having faith enough to listen is what will cause faith to grow into the place where we can please Him, as we obey what He says. We don't work to prove our faith, however, because we have faith we work.

Whenever we find ourselves in circumstances or tensions, and we don't understand, we must take our questions and turn them into worship. When we do this, our questions grow into trust. Trust is faith that has fully matured. The disciples had faith in the storm to pray to Jesus. Jesus had trust in His Father that everything was going to be just fine. Let God produce a sound mind in us, as it is renewed daily by the washing of His Word. The sound mind is simply a disciplined mind that believes God's word despite what it's eyes see.

The tension in Jesus' purpose in His earthly ministry is clearly seen when we have the mind of Christ. It is so interesting to see someone live in this tension perfectly. We should look unto Jesus and perceive that everything that He ever did could never be improved on. If we continue to look to Him, we will acquire a fascinated heart and a renewed mind. It is free, but it will cost us everything. The water of life is freely given, but when you count the cost of following the river, you may lose some friends who love the wilderness. Many people like the wilderness more than they should.

Look at these two verses that are absolutely true, but very different. *"For the Son of man is come to seek and to save that which was lost"* (Luke 19:10). *"For I am come to set a man at variance against his father, and the daughter against her mother, and the daughter in law against her mother in law"* (Matthew 10:35). One of these verses is in third person "For the Son of Man" and the other in first person "For I am come." They are written differently, but it's all working together to fulfill the Father's will. Only Jesus could fulfill these two objectives perfectly at the same time. Some people's prayers are crazy, they have tried to bind Jesus, which is foolish. Death and the grave were not even capable of such a thing of binding Jesus. Sometimes in prayer people speak peace to a war God Himself started. Jesus says, "I am the Resurrection and the Life." Yet He lays down His life and was resurrected by the Holy Spirit. In this tension, the knowledge of God and His ways are released. This makes me want to worship, while many others would like to debate. Some people in the body of Christ feel called to set everyone at variance; some feel called to seek and to save while they themselves are lost. This causes division. Jesus wasn't divided over this issue, for a divided kingdom cannot stand. His Kingdom knows no end and continues to increase; yet He never changes. He makes all things new but Himself. The tension in who God is and how He works is supposed to produce radical trust, which is what worship is. Worship is when we can see the beauty of the Lion and the Lamb. This tension can break our hearts and then we fully surrender our will and become like Christ. Then maybe God will be near. In our comfortable church pews we argue about the Bible as the whole world is on the way to hell. Meanwhile Jesus is knocking on the door, pursuing the lost people who like having church without Jesus. (see Revelation 3:19-20)

Seeing Jesus is the only cure for this horrible infection. It seems the church went for a vaccination of religion and got infected by the vaccine. However, Doctor Jesus is coming back around with a sword in His mouth and eye salve; we must choose the sword of His judgment or the mercy of eye salve so our eyes can see once again. Jesus is the only cure and Healer who can do anything, but we must let Him in the church again.

When you get to heaven, seeing Jesus changes everything. Just ask Daniel, Ezekiel, Elijah, Isaiah, and John the Revelator. *"But we see Jesus, who was made a little lower than the angels for the suffering of death, crowned with glory and honor; that by the grace of God should taste death for every man"* (Hebrew 2:9). Seeing Jesus is the audiences' common denominator, as they see Him, they see the suffering of death or the cross. They also see Him being crowned with glory and honor. These are two very important and different aspects to who Jesus really is. A suffering Savior who can drink death and come back to life, and a ruling King crowned with glory and honor. I am sure you see the tension again. Seeing Jesus for who He really is produces true change in us, this is the will of God. John the Revelator tells us that seeing Jesus is the only way real change occurs. *"Beloved, now we are the sons of God, and it doth not appear what we shall be: but we know that, when He shall appear, we shall be like Him; for we shall see Him as He is"* (1 John 3:2). You become what you behold. If you behold perverse pictures, you will become a pervert. However, if you behold the Lamb, you will become one accounted for the slaughter as Paul said.

Seeing Jesus will radically change you forever. The important part of seeing Jesus is not with our physical eyes, but with the eyes of our heart. Jesus said, "Blessed are those who have not seen and yet believed." The physical eyes are not the most important ingredients to see Jesus. Like the Pharisees, that only used their natural eyes and still couldn't see Him. Two blind men's cry was heard as they pleaded for mercy from the Son of David. *"And when Jesus departed thence, two blind men followed him crying, and saying, Thou son of David, have mercy on us"* (Matthew 9:27). What is awesome is the amount of revelation deeply contained in this short verse. First we see it is possible to follow Jesus blindly, just look at the church today, almost everyone's doing it. Then we see these men are not afraid to cry out and admit they are blind, many of Jesus' followers need to cry out in their blindness and get Jesus' attention. Jesus was not paying attention to their blindness, and they had to cry out in it to be healed of it. In this verse we also see if you need healing, you should speak to Jesus in King James, and then your healing will come, ha-ha. Now on a more serious note, these men through their need and blindness were able to recognize that Jesus was the fulfillment of prophecy. They knew He was the Son of David, yet they never read the scroll with their own eyes once. However their need and desperation for mercy enabled them by the grace of God to see who Jesus really was. The people who read and taught the scroll for a living, could not see Jesus! These men did not ask for healing, they asked for mercy and Jesus touched their eyes and gave them their sight. How exciting! The first person they ever saw was the sinless Lamb who had power to forgive sin and heal their health condition. Sickness is sin's health condition. Before sin entered the world there was no mention of sickness. Sin's vision is blindness. Religions health condition is blindness, deafness, dumbness, and lameness. The cross cures all the above.

These two men understood the Bible in a profound way, but they never read it. David said, "Surely goodness and mercy shall follow me." Jesus, David's Son and Savior said, "Signs and wonders follow those who believe." The attributes of God that release authentic miracles, or the character of true signs and wonders, are goodness and mercy. Through the mercy of God, these men received their healing. As we gaze upon Jesus together in the scripture, we will see different pictures of Him. These pictures of Him will bring us into the tension of who He really is. We will see a Lion and a Lamb, a throne and a cross. We will see a Jesus who flips over tables, and Jesus who weeps over Jerusalem the city where He flipped over tables. The most important thing is to see and hear Jesus. It is the beginning of success in the eyes of our God and Father. Success to the Father looks only like Jesus. Those who are truly successful or prosperous see, hear, touch, smell, and taste Jesus. True prosperity is being filled with the Spirit of God and overflowing on the world around us. We encounter Him until we receive from Him and become like Him. This takes us into authentic ministry, the ministry of doing what God says. Doing what God is saying is the only real Christianity that exists. Scripture has many pictures of Jesus; we will take a look at a few together. We touched this one previously but it's one of my favorites.

"He answered and said, Lo I see four men loose, walking in the midst of the fire, and they have no hurt; and the form of the fourth is like the Son of God" (Daniel 3:25).

Uncompromising devotion provoked Jesus to show Himself strong on the behalf of three young men. Now people see different things, when my pastor reads this verse he sees the people of God free and in the fire. He loves the sheep, so He notices what happens to the people. They were thrown in the fire bound, and then Jesus appears there and they are free, and walking. I see it in this way: Jesus doesn't even have to speak to free them from their bondage, and not only that, He doesn't even have to speak in the fire to deliver them from it. Even the smell of the fire is subject to His being. I also think this would have been a real good time for a charismatic altar call, but Jesus is absolutely silent in the fire according to scripture. That absolutely fascinates my heart, time and time again. I have laughed and cried thinking about it, even simultaneously done both. I love when the Holy Spirit gets a hold of you and you're laughing and crying at the same time, and there is no confusion on you, just peace and joy as God whacks you.

Let us look unto Jesus again, and remember He was in the midst of the fire.

Now see Jesus on water. Remember Jesus was silent in the fire.

"And when He was entered into a ship, His disciples followed Him. And, behold, there arose a great tempest in the sea, insomuch that the ship was covered with the waves: but He was asleep. And His disciples came to Him, and awoke Him, saying, Lord, save us: we perish. And He said unto them, Why are ye fearful, O ye of little faith? Then He arose, and rebuked the winds and the sea and there was a great calm" (Matthew 8:23-26).

You better believe the storm is going to come down when Jesus speaks to it. Yet that is not what Jesus was looking for in His disciples. As we focus on Jesus, we see Him sleeping in a storm He led them into. Similar to the fire that Jesus led the three young men into, as they kept His commandments and bowed to no other gods. He was silent in the fire, and now we see Jesus sleeping in the storm. It is quite interesting to find Jesus sleeping in the storm. For only a few verses earlier He said the Son of man had no place to lay His head, and then He's sleeping in the very next scene. Jesus is fully man, so He has to sleep, but He's fully God so He can sleep in a storm. If this were a movie it would be hilarious to everyone but those who were in the boat with Jesus. Many laugh from a distance, but some need to get in the boat with Jesus, and stop criticizing from the shore. Jesus would not have rebuked His disciples for not having enough faith, if they didn't have enough faith given by Him to rebuke the storm. They were given the faith because it comes by hearing, and all they had been doing is hearing the Word and seeing miracles. Faith comes by hearing but should stand in the power of God. The disciples are with the power of God, and it's clear that they have it, but don't remember it in the storm. Sometimes in trials we forget that we have been equipped to adequately deal with them, because grace is released in the time of need. In Luke, they ask Jesus a question that reveals what they believe about what is available to them. Check it out. *"And when His disciples James and John saw this, they said Lord, wilt thou that we command fire to come down from heaven, and consume them, even as Elijah did?"* (Luke 9:54). So they are not asking Jesus to call fire from heaven, they are asking Him if He would like them to. So, they can bring heaven to earth but they cannot calm a storm on earth. Jesus rebukes them. *"But He turned, and rebuked them, and said, Ye know not what manner of spirit ye are of. For the Son of Man is not come to destroy men's lives, but to save them. And they went to another village"* (Luke 9:55-56). The disciples took scripture out of context, didn't they?

Sometimes it is hard to see Jesus, when His words are not in some bibles. Jesus' words do not belong on the bottom of a page. If you look at the New International Version, you will find that scripture is missing. It was a Roman whip that took flesh from Jesus' back and Roman scholars who took words from the pages of this Book of Life we call the Bible. Jesus' words are spirit and life; none should be missing especially when He rebukes His disciples for acting the way humans are prone to act. They wanted to bring fire down on others; this was an old wine skin. I am not sure they were in-touch with what Jesus was doing, but they had a scripture reference to debate their cause with Jesus. However, they could not hear or see what the Father was doing, so they misused scripture. That happens all the time. Scripture is misused to verify people's wrong behavior. We need to see Jesus swiftly rebuke His disciples; an old wineskin may be another spirit. We must stay current with God.

Let's see Jesus a little more, concerning the boat and water. Jesus is praying and sees the disciples in the ship at risk, so He walks on the water to them. We will look at it from Matthew and Mark, there is much about this true story that can captivate and fascinate the human heart. The story is found in Matthew 14:22-33 and Mark 6:45-52, we have to put our eyes upon Jesus and focus on what He says and does carefully. It is crucial in the hour we live in, to keep our eyes on Jesus; it will keep our hearts from waxing cold. The disciples are in the boat without Jesus, and they see someone walking on the water and are afraid. Some of these men were fishermen, and it wasn't exactly normal to see people walking on the water. So when Jesus is doing something that is authentic to Him, He will identify what He's doing by His voice. Jesus said, "My sheep hear my voice and follow Me." So Peter did wind up following Him, and he walked on water. Here we see Jesus longing to be close to us. When He said, "come;" all twelve of the disciples could have gone to Him but only Peter did, he was hungry for Jesus. Jesus didn't say, "Peter come," He said, "come." He was speaking to twelve men, but only one of them heard Him. The one man who hears and obeys had a testimony, while eleven others had a story. Who will we be, the man with a testimony or the people with a story? When Peter saw the storm and was afraid he began to sink, and immediately Jesus caught Peter and lifted him up. Those who step out in the supernatural stand the chance of falling and sinking, but Jesus immediately sticks His hand out to catch us the way He did with Peter, because He is not a respecter of persons. The people in the boat never experienced walking on the water. Those who are in the boat of religion, without Jesus, tend to be critical of those who step out of a boat that Jesus is not in. I would have rather sunk trying to walk on the water, rather than die in a storm criticizing someone who started to walk on the water. The boat without Jesus is a clear picture of religion, and Peter walking on water shows the danger of walking in the supernatural and the saving grace of the Lord. Who did Jesus save first is the question? Who did Jesus touch first, Peter or the boat of un-believing believers? Good answer, Peter. Peter actually became part of the solution to those in the boat who were sinking. Simply walking with Jesus, makes us part of the solution. *"And when they were come into the ship, the wind ceased"* (Matthew 14:32). *"And He went up unto them into the ship; and the wind ceased: and they were sore amazed in themselves beyond measure, and wondered"* (Mark 6:51).

On one account Jesus is sleeping in the storm. On another account He doesn't even speak to the storm, He simply gets in the boat and the storm stops. Jesus is someone you cannot box into your head. You cannot make religious rules to think you know what Jesus is going to do, you never know with Him. It is glorious to serve a God who is full of mysteries, yet He Himself knows all things.

Jesus didn't only reach out to Peter immediately, He also reached out to His disciples who were afraid because they were seeing something they never saw before. When God is doing something we have never seen before, it can be identified by His voice. He didn't want them to be afraid or deceived, so immediately He identified what they saw by His voice and He will do the same for us. The gospel of Mark shows this very well; *"And He saw them toiling in rowing; for the wind was contrary unto them: and about the fourth watch of the night He cometh unto them, walking upon the sea, and would have passed by them. But when they saw Him walking upon the sea, they supposed it had been a spirit, and cried out: For they saw Him, and were troubled. And immediately He talked with them, and said unto them, Be of good cheer it is I; be not afraid"* (Mark 6:48-50). Immediately He responded to them, this reveals His infinite kindness to the sincere.

Scripture says, "They saw him and were troubled." Seeing Jesus at times will trouble you. David said it like this, *"I remembered God, and was troubled"* (Psalm 77:3a). Later in the text, the scripture speaks of the condition of the disciples' hearts. "For their heart was hardened." That word hardened means a kind of stone, petrified, callous, blind, or to render stupid. This is describing the heart that does not see Jesus or consider His previous miracles. The previous miracles should have helped their hard hearts soften up a little. The disciples didn't remember that Jesus just supernaturally fed 5,000 by the obedience of their faith.

Seeing and hearing Jesus must be our main priority. Jesus is silent in the fire, He walks on the water, He sleeps in the storm, and when He speaks peace the storm stops. I could never explain how amazing Jesus really is.

We will see Jesus a little more together, in another chapter. It is awesome to just focus on Jesus, be still and know that He is God. He is completely good, and His plans for us are better than any plans we could ever devise ourselves. His plans are good even sometimes when everything doesn't always feel good. Sometimes seeing Jesus may trouble us, and following Jesus may get us in trouble. Yet He doesn't lead us into something He is not going to be with us in, and see us through. He sees us. The question is do we see Him? Do we have pure hearts or petrified hearts? A Pure heart sees God. Hearts that are alive see Jesus, and who He really is. A pure heart remembers what Jesus did on the cross thousands of years ago, and what He did last week in our life and family. Pure hearts must forgive those who wrong them, or their hearts won't stay very pure for long. Forgiveness is one of the languages God speaks. He manifested that language from Calvary as He prayed from the cross, "Father forgive them." A pure heart is a tender heart that forgives those who have wronged them and remembers what God had done for them. We need to forget what people have done to us and remember what God has done for us. If we do this and give our attention to what He is saying, we will live a powerful Spirit filled life.

We have seen some interesting pictures of Jesus. From this, we have learned that He doesn't even have to speak for things to happen. We learned that when He speaks, storms stop immediately. The Word of His power is stunning and beyond understanding to the carnal mind. Thank God for the mind of Christ. Jesus paid for us to have the mind of Christ by His crown of thorns. We need the mind of Christ to even begin to touch on such matters concerning the manifestation of the Word of His power.

> *"Hath in these last days spoken unto us by His Son, whom He hath appointed heir of all things, by whom also He made the worlds; Who being the brightness of His glory, and the express image of His person, and upholding all things by the word of His power, when He purged our sins, sat down on the right hand of the Majesty on high"* (Hebrews 1:2-3).

The Father speaks through the Son. The Father opens His mouth and Jesus comes out. Jesus is the visible light that shines off of the invisible God who is our Father. We come through the Son, into relationship with the Father and are no longer orphans. The Spirit of Adoption has purchased us and desires to posses us with the cry for our "Abba Father." Jesus is a perfect reflection of our Father. Jesus said, "If you have seen Me, you have seen the Father." This truth causes the writer of Hebrews to say that Jesus is the "brightness of His glory, and the express image of His person." The Father not only created all things through the Son, but also upholds all things by the Word of His power. He is the creator and sustainer of all things. While Jesus was dead in a tomb for three days, the creative order of this cosmos stayed exactly where He left it. The earth and the world could not do anything contrary to what Jesus said when He created it, and placed it where He desired it to be. Jesus' government was increasing even while blood was leaking out of His body on the cross. While Jesus was being ripped apart by a cat-of-nine tails, His word was holding all things together.

The power of His Word is seen and manifested in so many different ways, it is stunning. The Word has power to create and up hold. It has power to create something out of nothing. There is healing in the spoken Word. The Word that is heard produces faith. The Word is a discerner of the thought and the intents of the heart. The Word is a judge of what we do and why we do it. The Word of the Lord made the heavens. The Word is like a hammer, because it will break you. The Word is like a fire, because it will consume you. The water of the Word will wash us. The Word is a lamp unto our feet and a light unto our path. Think about that, it would be like saying that water is like the plastic bottle and the water that it contains. The lamp is where the light shines from. The Word of Jesus is the place the light shines from, and He is the light, and we are in Him. The One we live in guides us.

The Lord watches over His word; *"Then said the Lord unto me, thou hast well seen: for I will hasten my word to perform it"* (Jeremiah 1:12). In the verse before it, the Lord tested his sight and asked Jeremiah what he saw, so the Word of the Lord tested him. The Lord was motivated to hasten or to be on the look out, watch over, to be sleepless to perform His word. The Word of God is living and active. It can watch over itself. The Word that tests us prepares us for the Word to perform itself, while it is watching over itself and holding all things together simultaneously.

We see this principal in action with Joseph. Joseph had a word from God that came in a dream, and his word had a season. Psalm 105:17 tells us it is Joseph we are talking about, and Psalm 105:19 tells us what is needed to hear and see. *"Until the time that His word came: the word of the Lord tried or melt, refine, purge away, him."* The word tests us and prepares us, and in do season it comes to us. The Word is living and it has the ability to watch over itself and get the self out of us, all at the same time.

The power of His word is seen when Jesus speaks the word and the centurion's servant was healed. This story can be found in Matthew 8:5-10. The word heals, strengthens, and even resurrects. Lazarus was dead for four days. Jesus with a loud voice said "Lazarus come forth." Jesus had to say, *"Lazarus* come forth" or the whole graveyard would have awoken out of their tombs. Remember Jesus is the resurrection and the life and when He speaks it happens exactly how He says it.

The power of His word touches the souls of men, and can wholly posses the soul of man. God's word should control how we feel if we are truly mature in Him. When the word of the Lord posses us, we can experientially say "amen" to what Jeremiah experienced. "Thy word was the rejoicing of my heart." This is Jeremiah saying that God's word is the climate control of his heart. What God says is what should control how we feel, if Jesus is really the Lord of our life. Ezekiel's wife died and this is what God said to him. *"Son of man, behold, I take away from thee the desire of thine eyes with a stroke: yet neither shalt thou mourn nor weep, neither shall thy tears run down. Forbear to cry, make no mourning for the dead, bind the tire of thine head upon thee, and put on thy shoes upon thy feet, and cover not thy lips, and eat not the bread of men. So I spake unto the people in the morning: and at even my wife died; and I did in the mourning as I was commanded"* (Ezekiel 24:16-18). This is a great picture of a man being possessed by God's word even when it's not comfortable for him. Ezekiel loved God more than his feelings. This is a great picture of what "first love" looks like. If he would have cried he would have disobeyed. He didn't because the Word was in his heart and it kept him from sin. The words of the Psalmist really apply well to Ezekiel right here. "Thy word have I hid in my heart that I might not sin against you." Jesus, in Matthew 4, spoke the word that He gave Moses in Deuteronomy 6 to Satan and he had to flee. Submission to God and His word causes the enemy to flee.

God's word doesn't only keep us from sin, but it separates us or consecrates us for righteousness sake. Jesus said, *"sanctify them through thy truth for thy word is truth"* (John 17:17). Before Jesus was crucified He was thinking about you being separated for Him alone. We might hear more about American Idol in church than we do about sanctification. Sanctification was on Jesus' mind and so it should be on ours also, if we have the mind of Christ. When the Holy Spirit leads us, we are sanctified for Christ Jesus' good pleasure alone. A lot of the church is in bed with the world, but God is saying, "Come out of her." The Holy Spirit reminds us of what Jesus has said while leading us directly and continually into His presence. It is God's voice that leads us to Him. A great picture of this truth is Peter walking on the water to Jesus. Jesus said come, and it brought Peter closer to Him. His voice draws us to Himself. His "rhema" word brought Peter into an encounter with the "Logos" word, called Him.

Holy Spirit will lead us to do what Jesus is praying and saying; this is called the will of God or the heavenly calling, which is in Christ Jesus. Jesus prays the Father's will and the Holy Spirit leads sons on the journey of pleasing the Father. This process is the will of God. The Spirit of God quickens us by the Word that proceeds from the Father's mouth, called Jesus. When the Lord Jesus speaks, there is grace that His words are seasoned with, that releases the ability to fulfill and obey what He has commanded. God gives us grace so that we can walk in the truth. Grace unmerited favor. Mercy is not getting what we deserve; grace is getting what we don't deserve. Mercy picks us up when we fall, grace causes us to stand. Jesus came full of grace and truth. When He speaks about His attributes, those attributes are imparted to us. When Jesus speaks to us, He's actually forming Himself in us.

The Word is a person; Jeremiah called Him, "the Word of the Lord." Many times Jeremiah said, "The Word of the Lord came to me." Jesus revealed Himself to John as the "Word of God." The Word of God is deeper and more relevant to everyday life than we know. It is a great privilege for us to have the Holy Scriptures. The Word of God, who is a person, came down off His throne and died on a cross for us. So you have the Word dying on a tree. What's pretty interesting is His words wind up on a dead tree for us to read. Paper is a dead tree, but it becomes living when God's Word is put on it. I can't express my gratitude enough for the countless men and women, who were martyred and burned on the stake so we can have the very words of an unfailing, and infallible God. There is no other book like the Bible because it is all true.

Jesus, we have learned, is the Word of the Lord that appeared to Elijah; we know the Word is a person. In the book of Revelation describes Jesus in so many ways, but there is something specific I want to put our eyes on. *"And when I saw Him, I fell at His feet as dead. And He laid His right hand upon me, saying unto me, Fear not, I am the first and the last: I am He that liveth, and was dead; and behold. I am alive for evermore. Amen; and have the keys of hell and of death. Write these things which thou hast seen, and these things which are and the things which shall be here after"* (Revelation 1:17-19). John is becoming "John the

Revelator" as he falls at Jesus' feet. He is not seeing Jesus' feet pierced and dripping blood, he's seeing feet like burnished brass. Then Jesus starts speaking to John. Jesus says something personal to John about His eternal existence. "I am He that liveth, and was dead, and am alive forever more." In Revelation 1:8, we see something similar: *"I am Alpha and Omega, the beginning and the ending, saith the Lord, which was, and which is, and which is to come, the Almighty."* This is the person of the Word, Jesus the Alpha and the Omega. Jesus is revealing Himself to John in a way that John has never seen before; in a place He has never been before and using a name He has never referred to Himself by before. There are three timings to who He is. The One who was, the One who is, and the One who is to come. "I am He that liveth and was dead and am alive forevermore." This is the person of the Word, and if we are ever going to understand the words that He speaks we are going to have to get acquainted with the Jesus who was and the Jesus who is and the Jesus who is to come. A good theology does not only know Jesus as it relates to His earthy ministry, even though He constantly brought heaven to earth. Sound theology is to know the Jesus who was, the Jesus who in the beginning created the world, and the Jesus who is the beginning. It is necessity to know the Jesus who was dead and is now alive, the pierced and resurrected Jesus, the One who opens the Scripture and causes men's hearts to burn. We must know the Jesus with fire in His eyes and a sword in His mouth. The Christ whose death could not hold; the Jesus who will come on a white horse and make war on the earth; the Jesus who arises with healing in His wings; the Jesus who identifies Himself with the least of these; the Jesus whose vesture is dipped in blood, whose name is the "Word of God." To know the Jesus who was and who is and who is to come is sound theology. It is not enough to know the Jesus of the four gospels, if it were, He would not have revealed Himself to John the Revelator the way He did in the book of Revelation. This will cause us to tremble at His word, then He will build His home in us and we will truly be His fragrance in the earth. This revelation of Jesus is what is going to bring the fear of the Lord back to the church once again. His word has to find residence in us if Jesus is going to be preeminent in our lives.

The understanding of the Word as a person is necessary for intimacy with God. As well as radical obedience to what He has revealed in His word, and is saying to us by His Spirit presently. When He speaks and reveals His word, it is necessary to know that His word has timing to it. In the western world, we make plans with a person for when we are going to meet with them. Well, so it is with the Word of God. It has a time and a season in which it will manifest. It is so hard to even begin to understand the timing of the Word of the Lord without knowing the Word Himself and allowing Him to live in and through us.

The Word touches faith and we then have conception of the seed of the Word Himself living in us. Christ in us is the only way that it is possible for full comprehension of the timing of the Word. This understanding comes to us as we mature. The mind of Christ is how we prove the will of God according to the scriptures, but it is the Holy Spirit who helps us to know the when of God's word. The timing of the Word will bring tension also. Remember the Word is a person and He has a day and it is great and terrible. This is obviously a great tension, hence great for some and terrible for others. This day is coming soon to a planet near you; no man knows the day or the hour. The Great and Terrible day, has a timing to it and only the Father knows when He will send His Son to return for a bride that is without spot or wrinkle. So this day, that is great and terrible, has a timing and no physical day or hour is known or given, but the tension of the day is very clear to see that it is near.

The timing of the Word is such an interesting topic, because the Word is eternal. Heaven and earth will pass away but His Word will not pass away as everything else does. When Jesus died His word held the planet in motion, which held His dead body in the tomb, so He could be raised from the dead. Truly He has exalted His "Word above His own name." For three days when He was dead and would not respond to the name Jesus, His word held all things together. Truly there is no one like Him.

If Abraham had not heard the Word of the Lord while Isaac was on the altar, it is life or death to hear or be deaf. Not only does our life depend on it, but the lives of others. If God doesn't touch us how can we touch them? If we don't hear God, how can we tell them? The soul of man's timing is now; the timing of God is waiting. Paul tells young Timothy, *"study to show thyself approved unto God, a workman that needeth not to be ashamed, rightly dividing the word of truth"* (2 Timothy 2:15). Approved of God, not man; approved to God, not elected by man. God's Kingdom is not a democracy. It is a supreme, holy and loving monarchy, where the King has our best interests in mind, from eternity to eternity. Paul tells Timothy to rightly divide the word of Truth, but in Hebrews Paul later says the *"Word of God is quick and powerful, and sharper than any two-edged sword, piercing even to the dividing asunder of soul and spirit, and of joints and marrow, and is a discerner of the thoughts and intents of the heart"* (Hebrews 4:12).

Paul teaches Timothy to rightly divide something that will rightly divide him. Paul is telling this young Apostle, Timothy to study something that will study him. The Word is living and will discern your thoughts and intents. An example of our thoughts would be what we think or do, and our intents would be why we think or do something. As the Word is dividing our soul and spirit, it is then that discernment grows and deepens in us. As this happens, we then begin to understand the timing of the Word. While the

Word is dividing us in a good way, we then begin to understand the timing of the Word.

I like to say it like this; the Word has seven layers and three timings. The Jesus who was, who is, and who is to come, is the timing. *"The words of the Lord are pure words: as silver tried in the furnace of the earth, purified seven times"* (Psalm 12:6). Those words were perfect and pure before they even went into the furnace, what about after? Not one of those words will ever pass away or not come to pass. When we stand on the Word, the Word Himself will show up for us.

"Then was Nebuchadnezzar full of fury, and the form of his visage was changed against Shadrach, Meshach, and Abednego: therefore he spake, and commanded that they should heat the furnace one seven times hotter than it was wont to be heated" (Daniel 3:19). The Babylonians heat the furnace seven times hotter and the Word Himself shows up in the furnace. The Hebrew boys didn't compromise God's word or law, and they were thrown into the furnace. Have you ever done the right thing and got the wrong results. This same thing happened to Joseph, he didn't sleep with Potiphar's wife and he got thrown in prison. The Word was with them in the fire and with Joseph in the prison. Jesus was silent but visible; do we see Jesus in the fiery trials of life? Or are we blind to Him when He is silent? The Word of the Lord tested Joseph as it did to the three Hebrew boys. They had God's Word hidden in their hearts, therefore they did not sin against Him as the scriptures teach in Psalms. When the Word of God is truly hidden in our hearts, Christ becomes visible to others in our lives. When we stand up for the Word, He shows up for us. Perhaps Babylon wouldn't have seen Jesus if three young men wouldn't have kept His word. What happened here is what Jesus promised in the Gospel of John. *"He that hath my commandments, and keepeth them, he it is that loveth me: and he that loveth me shall be loved of my Father, and I will love him, and will*

manifest myself to him" (John 13:21). They kept the word and He kept His promise to manifest or reveal Himself. That is a great picture of what real Christianity is.

The Word that tests us is the Word that refines us, and makes us pure and prepares us.

It is very biblical to ask ourselves questions. We must test ourselves and judge ourselves to see if we are in the Faith. Faith comes by hearing the Word of God, if we abide in Him, then His words will abide in us, and then we will have wealth that will endure fervent heat. True riches can endure fervent heat, but temporary riches solve temporary problems. When earthly money is given wisely, true riches are stored up in heaven and go before the Lord as a memorial (see Acts 10). When we are poor in spirit we receive access to the riches of His grace.

The Word of the Lord has timing and it is perfect. The Word was God, and the Word with God, and He created all things. The Word is forever settled in heaven, yet He is coming soon, on a white horse, with the armies of heaven behind Him. His Word can be forever settled yet He is on the move. I love the beautiful tension we live in; it is in it where we find the will of God on the narrow road. The Kingdom of God is continually increasing, yet the King never changes. Truly the wisdom of God is a mystery. The Lord Jesus builds and creates by His Word. He sanctifies, saves, and heals by His Word. He is the Word who became flesh, and was ripped apart, so we can be mended and whole. He had no place to rest His head, so that we could rest our head upon His chest. His Word must be our hope, or we will become hopeless. He builds and empowers by His Word, we can only please Him by obeying the word that He speaks, which is seasoned with lots of grace and empowers us for the work of faith with power. He keeps us in truth and allows us to stand for Him and His purposes.

"Whom shall He teach knowledge? And who shall He make to understand doctrine? Them that are weaned from the milk, and drawn from the breasts. For precept must be upon precept; precept upon precept; line upon line, line upon line; here a little there a little" (Isaiah 28:9-10). "Them" are the covenant people of God that would not listen, and we still are living in the same conditions only worse. There is only one remedy for us and it is the cross of Jesus Christ. We also must return to the Lord with fasting and praying, and then listening and obeying. If we fast and pray and don't listen and obey, we become like the people in Isaiah 58 who "take joy in approaching God" but are disconnected to what is truly on His heart. (see Isaiah 58)

So the Lord builds by precept or command, and it empowers us to do what He wants, and not what we want. For example, He gives two commandments: Love God with everything, and love your neighbor as yourself. There were Ten Commandments, but ten divided by two = love those who you see and love a God who you might not see with your eyes until you breathe your last breath. I call this Holy Spirit algebra. Holy Spirit math class will always cause us to behave like Jesus. The only way to fulfill the great commission is by these two commandments. Commandment in the Greek is used in these verses where Jesus is telling us to love God, and commandment literally means prescription. The commandments or prescriptions of the Lord are the only way possible to fulfill the Great Commission. Many people put the horse before the cart and try to work before their heart is set on love. This only leads to burn out and unhealthy relationships and unnecessary church splits. Here is the Great Commission: "Go into all the World and preach the Gospel." It doesn't say build a huge building with lots of lights, get into lots of debt and manipulate people for money weekly in the name of Jesus. It doesn't say pray the gospel and run from God's commission to preach. It doesn't say become a civil rights activist. It doesn't say start a Christian band. All of that is great but the first thing must remain first, or we are out of order. First, it says love God, then love people, and then preach the Gospel. Pray without ceasing, pray all night, which I love to do with lots of coffee, but don't be silent outside. Love cannot stay silent, and real fire cannot stay locked up in your bones or in a building, just ask Jeremiah. *"Then I said, I will not make mention of Him, nor speak any more in His name. But His word was in mine heart as a burning fire shut up in my bones, and I was weary with forbearing, and I could not stay"* (Jeremiah 20:9). If you really know Jesus, it is impossible not to make Him known. There is no possible way that you can know the way and not tell others who are lost. Fire cannot be contained, it can only consume. It will consume you and when you are no more. It will have to come out of you, the Word never returns void. The Spirit of God was moving, and the earth was void, but when God spoke, light came and the earth was no longer void. Void is the absence of substance, but we know that the substance of faith comes by hearing, and the earth and the atmosphere itself must hear when the Word speaks. Not only did the nothing that didn't exist before God spoke, but that same nothing had to become something, and God called it good. The creative building capability of the Word of the Lord is stunning.

The Lord Jesus' faith is framed out in us as He speaks. One day in the spirit of my mind, that is supposed to be renewed daily, I saw a picture. The picture came to the eyes of my understanding or imagination. It was "gold two by fours." So I said, "Holy Spirit, what is that?" Then He said, "I am building a home for Myself in you." I was messed up and winded up in tears having no idea what this really meant. Afterwards I remembered that Jesus was a carpenter on earth, a wise Master Builder, and so glad He wasn't asking me to do it but rather showing me what He was doing. When we learn what the Lord is doing, we then learn to participate but not get in His way by trying to do it ourselves. This took a lot of pressure off me. Besides I was a plumber by trade, and building certainly wasn't a strong suite of mine. I learned a cool lesson one-day plumbing. It was freezing cold and I was doing some plumbing work in the basement of a huge house in New Jersey. I was soldering. For those who do not know, the metal has to become hot enough to melt into an almost liquid state, for the joint to be sealed properly. So I overheated the copper pipe, and all of a sudden I saw a perfect rainbow. So then plumbing goes out the window briefly, and I hear the Holy Spirit start asking me questions. "Where does copper come from?" So I say, "the earth, Lord." He says, "good." Then the Lord basically says, "did you see what just happened?" "Yes" I said, and then I stopped plumbing for a minute. Then I heard a whisper, "when My fire touches something earthen, a token of covenant must manifest." So then I partially began to understand what He was speaking about. Before the throne of God, there are seven lamps; lamps are for light. These are the Seven Spirits of God, and above the throne you have a rainbow with seven colors. Remember the lamps before the throne are for light. After the fire of God purifies you, covenant is established. The earth was judged and then the God made a covenant with Noah, and the rainbow was its token. The homosexual agenda has tried to twist the rainbow and make it a gay flag. It will never be that, no one can redefine what God has already defined. The rainbow is first called "My bow" by God in Genesis 9:13. This is God's bow and will always be God's bow. It is a token of covenant; covenant is with God and man, and men and women. Anything else is false and profane in the sight of a Holy God. There are two types of fire that come from Heaven; the fire that makes gold, and causes covenant to be seen, and the fire that burnt Sodom and Gomorrah to ashes - your choice friend. The fire of His Word is coming to a remnant that seeks His face continually. The fire is uncontainable and all consuming. So if it is really there, it will have to come out. Just like a river cannot help but flow, that is what rivers do. The Word of God, talks about rivers flowing from our belly in John 7:38. We take a drink and it becomes a river, how is that for math. What can fit in a cup, cannot even be contained or described properly in one river, but to describe it better the plural word "rivers" is used. In the Old Testament we are planted by the streams of living water, in the New Covenant the rivers flow from us to them.

Jesus was not into self-help; He was into self-denial. Meaning we deny ourselves and He reveals Himself. He has never changed His mind, because He is the same yesterday, today and forever. If He were ever in some churches, where all self-help books are, He might exercise His self-control by flipping over their book tables. Perhaps if He showed up in modern day apparel, He might take His belt off and beat a few pastors and deacons for corrupting the house of the Lord with self-help. He might look at what He shed His precious blood for and weep, as He sees us drowning in apathy, and while complacency is strangling the people of God. Jesus was not into self-help; He was into us denying ourselves, and taking up our cross. If we don't hear, follow, and obey Him, we are simply not Christians. I don't care what prayer you prayed, or who told you what a Christian is. For a real Christian is someone who loves and obeys Jesus.

Jesus does not give His disciples a whole lot of stuff to do, and confuse them. He basically says love God, love people, preach the Gospel, and take heed that no man deceive you. It is simple, but we make it more complicated than it is. The deeper God's river drowns us, and the more God's fiery word burns in us, the more we see Jesus according to scripture. Then we become less focused on self, and on other people's opinions of us. The opinion that really matters is Jesus'. At the end of the day, it is His opinion that really matters.

Jesus said to "be" something, and it absolutely interested me, to the point of having more coffee to keep a late night study going. The intrigue of Jesus telling us to "be" something grabbed my heart and mind. I had a feeling some things were soon to be squeezed out of heart and knocked out of my mind. Sure enough I was right. That's one in a row!

Jesus said in Matthew 10:16 *"be ye therefore wise"* — the verse continues. However, I am using this statement to illustrate that Jesus wants us to become something. He does not just want us to do something, but also rather become something. Paul puts language to it, as well as David and Solomon. It is important to be what Jesus says to be, because you can only know Jesus and serve Him on His terms. I am emphasizing scripture a lot, because Jesus did. Also, in this generation especially, I have seen a lack of reverence for scripture. This is a generation who desperately needs to approach the scriptures with the mind of Christ. There is a last day's deception going on and perhaps it is fueled by the lack of reverence for God's word, and His house and how His people are treated. Jeremiah said we can "see the Word of the Lord." God is searching the earth for a company who fear Him, and tremble at His word. Those are the people who can see what God is saying and doing. The Lord truly desires to show Himself strong on the behalf of those who are both friendly toward Him and fearful of Him. The fear of the Lord is the beginning of wisdom, and wisdom is what should guide our decisions. Our decisions are a reflection of who we really are. That is why someone who commits adultery is an adulterer, or someone who lies is a liar.

In the Word of God there are many interesting things, but something specifically that is profound. It is how Paul puts language, expression, and structure to many of the things Jesus said. It is awesome to see the humility of our God, and how He would use Paul, after he spent a lifetime persecuting the church. When I think of Paul, I know that many Muslims will come to Jesus and know He is the Son of God and that He is Lord of all. Look at what Paul says to young Timothy; *"But continue thou in the things which thou hast learned and hast been assured of, knowing whom thou hast learned them; And that from a child thou hast known the Holy Scriptures, which are able to make thee wise unto salvation through Faith in Jesus Christ. All Scripture is given by inspiration of God, and is profitable for doctrine, for reproof, for correction, for instruction in righteousness: That the man of God may be perfect, thoroughly furnished unto all good works"* (2 Timothy 3:14-17). The Holy Scripture literally is able, through Jesus Christ, to make us wise unto salvation. The scriptures not only tell you to work out your salvation with fear and trembling, but teach you how through the operation of the Holy Spirit to do it. During this process we become what Jesus tells us to be, "wise." Wise men hear their Fathers words; wise men win souls. Wise virgins have oil in their lamps. A wise son makes his Father glad. There are many things wise men do, but the scripture makes us able, through Jesus Christ, to be wise. It is important because Jesus commanded it, and His command, is our commission and privilege. The Holy Spirit's name is Comforter, He does the convicting, but He is the Comforter. He reminds us of Jesus' words and leads us into all truth. The Holy Spirit leads us into the depths of Jesus Christ. Wisdom flows from a wise person. God is all wise and all knowing, so out of His mouth comes wisdom. When the Father opens His mouth and speaks, Jesus comes out, for He is the wisdom of God. We become wise as we give our ears to hearing Jesus. The scriptures are very essential in following Jesus on His terms. The Pharisees, Scribes, and Sadducees read the scriptures, they all even read the same version, but they did not know the Author when He was standing before them. They read with no hearing or seeing of the Author Himself. This was tragic to their eternal destiny. However, it is crucial for Jesus' true followers to be able to recognize Jesus through the scriptures. Our image of Jesus must not be how we want to see Him or what society or even church culture describes Him to be. It is absolutely crucial that we can recognize Jesus for who He is according to His word. Being deceived is not limited to not knowing what is not of God, but it is also not recognizing God in motion. Even worldly people know what is not of God. Discernment is being able to recognize Jesus when He comes in another form, we will touch this more later. Discernment is not merely to recognize who and what is not of God, but to recognize who is and what is of God.

When Andrew found Jesus, he heard Him referred to as the Lamb of God. According to what John the Baptist said in John 1:36. Then we hear Andrew reveal his understanding of the scripture, because Andrew heard that Jesus was the Lamb of God. So he heard a prophetic word, from the most prominent prophetic ministry of that day, and was able to apply it to scripture. Andrew goes on to say something else; *"He first findeth his own brother Simon, and said unto him, we have found the Messiah, which is interpreted, the Christ"* (John 1:41). John prophesies, they believe and put scripture to it. John did not say He was the Christ, but he said, "Behold the Lamb of God," and they did. It obviously hit them that this is the Christ. John did not call Him the Christ, but Andrew did. If Andrew was not familiar with the scriptures he would not have known what John the Baptist was really saying. We see this again even more plainly a few verses later.

Peter joins Jesus' ministry team after receiving a word of knowledge concerning his name. When Jesus said to Peter, without being introduced formally, "Thou art Simon the son of Jonas: thou shalt be called Cephas." The Word Himself gives Peter a word of knowledge, and so Peter is now a follower. The prophecy or command of John saying, "Behold the Lamb of God" caused Andrew to follow. Not only that but to get Peter, who is apprehended by a word of knowledge. Jesus apprehends people differently, and it is so beautiful to see Jesus apprehend a follower His way. We always want formulas, but Jesus only does and says what He sees and hears the Father say and do. The reason we like formulas is so we can do it without God. Many times we are like Adam and Eve trying to make our own covering.

Jesus calls Philip, and Philip finds Nathanael, and describes whom he has found in an interesting way; *"Philip findeth Nathanael, and saith unto him, We have found him, of whom Moses in the Law, and the prophets did write, Jesus of Nazareth, the son of Joseph"* (John 1:45). Philip gave proof, concerning Jesus, through the written word of Moses and in the prophets. The point is that there were several different authors. So from the scriptures, Philip gives Nathanael enough for him to know that this is He, this is Jesus of Nazareth. Jesus only at this point said two words to Philip, "Follow Me," and Philip is already evangelizing. Already looking for their friends to come also, these men did not have to go to one evangelism training session. Two words from Jesus and they are looking for the lost. Jesus' followers knew the scriptures before they even meet Him. That is why they could recognize Him. They were wise unto salvation, due to that when they saw Salvation they followed Him. Christ must be first recognized for who He is, if we are going to really follow Him. John the Baptist told them to "Behold the Lamb." He did not say anything about following Him, but it comes natural to those who behold Him. What is interesting to see, is man's view of what God is doing. Philip says to Nathanael, "we have found Him," speaking about Jesus. This is a classic picture of how man views what God is doing, and how man interprets the move of God. We sometimes don't think or see it, but Jesus on earth was the move of God, for He was God moving in the earth accomplishing His Father's will perfectly. How could He do everything perfect if He was not Himself? Simple - He couldn't, which shows His divinity very clearly. We can only be what we are, we can only give what we are. He was perfect therefore He did everything perfectly.

Nathanael says to Philip, "we have found Him." Was Jesus lost? Or did Jesus come to seek and save what was lost? Men without Jesus are lost, no matter how good they are, no matter how moral or immoral, anyone without Jesus is lost. So Nathanael says we found Jesus, but Jesus said to Nathanael, "follow me." Jesus did not say to Nathanael, thanks for finding Me! Jesus also did not ask him to go get Philip. This becomes natural. Bringing others to Jesus is natural because He is that good.

Just in a little bit of scripture in John chapter one, we see people call Jesus different names. John the Baptist calls Him the Lamb of God, Andrew calls Him Rabbi, and Andrew says to Peter we have found the Messiah or the Anointed One. The interesting thing is that scripture does not directly tell us who even saw Jesus as the Holy Spirit baptized Him. Philip identifies Jesus as Jesus of Nazareth, son of Joseph. Nathanael calls Him Rabbi, the Son of God, and the King of Israel. The scriptures paint pictures of Jesus. Scripture is about seeing Him and becoming wise, as He commanded. The life of Christ, and the scriptures, has something in common. It is this, they are both true and cannot lie. All of Jesus' words shall come to pass, just like Jesus will come again. The Word is pursuing us and praying for us daily. Jesus' prayer empowers us to know Him because it is His desire to know us, for He loved us first. Scripture, and the life of Jesus, brings such a tension that breaks our hearts, so that God would be near to us. It was God's idea to tell us to draw near to Him and He will draw near to us. The scriptures are to bring us into an encounter with a Living God, not to give us good points to argue while hell opens up and swallows lost humanity. When Jesus went into His ministry, He read the scriptures where He said, "The Spirit of the Lord is upon Me because He has anointed Me to preach the gospel." Then He goes on to say, "Scripture is fulfilled in your ears." This marks the beginning of His ministry, and then at the end of His earthly ministry, we see Jesus waiting for the timing of scripture to be fulfilled.

While Jesus, the Word who became flesh, was ripped apart and hanging from a tree, bleeding profusely, He still knew something. It was concerning the scriptures, and this is important to catch. Even while Jesus is offering up His life, He is doing it by the book because He was the Author and Finisher of it.

This is taking place while Jesus is on the tree. *"After this, Jesus knowing that all things were now accomplished, that the scripture might be fulfilled, said, I thirst"* (John 19:28). While Jesus is dying, there is a timing that has to come before He could have even said He was thirsty. While the Son of God is hanging, and every fiber of His being is being stretched to the very max, it all must be done in the timing and the order of scripture. To see Jesus hanging for us and becoming subject to His own words, may allow us to see the privilege we have of adhering to the scriptures and even dying God's way. The scriptures are able to make us wise unto salvation and even teach us the time to speak and not to speak, as the Holy Spirit leads us. There is a time to speak and a time to be silent according to Ecclesiastes. Wise people know what to, and what not to say. They know when to and when not to speak, who to and who not to speak to.

The Psalmist's advises us to be wise; *"Be wise now therefore, O ye kings: be instructed, ye judges of the earth. Serve the Lord with fear, and rejoice with trembling. Kiss the Son, lest He be angry, and ye perish from the way, when His wrath is kindled but a little. Blessed are all they that put their trust in Him"* (Psalm 2:10-12).

The Son is the One who says, "be ye therefore wise." Know that the psalmist is telling us to kiss the Son, lest you perish from the way. Jesus is the Son, Jesus is the way, and He is the one who told us to be wise. His word gives us the knowledge of how, and His Spirit quickens us to make it happen. Jesus and His Word are inseparable, just as love and truth, or the Father and the Son are inseparable. Reverence for the Word, and earnest desire for the Spirit's operation are inseparable. Error comes to those who do not know the scriptures or the power of God. *"Do ye not therefore err, because ye know not the scriptures, neither the power of God?"* (Matthew 12:24). The Holy Spirit baptizes the Word. When the Spirit baptized Jesus at the river Jordan, the Father spoke a word to the Word Himself. Peter preaches the word and the people are filled with the Holy Spirit. Jesus the Word, was anointed to preach. It is impossible not to tell people about Jesus, if you have spent time with the real Jesus. The real Jesus being the Jesus of the Bible, the Jesus who hung on a cross and waited for scripture to be fulfilled and then said, I thirst, leading to "it is finished," referring to the cup and our purchase. The Word establishes us and the Spirit moves us, the only wind a Christian should be moved by, is the wind of God.

The wind of God comes from His very breath; the word of God is the sound that His breath creates when He thinks out loud. He gave us the mind of Christ for when He doesn't think out loud. It is crucial that we come to the scriptures with the mind of Christ, so we can see Jesus.

Earlier the topic was brought up, that scripture should lead you to an encounter with God. I really believe what I wrote, because scriptures show it very clearly. His voice should draw us into His presence. In both Old and New Testaments this concept is visible if we have eyes to see. Daniel, Shadrach, Meshach, and Abednego all kept the law of God and did not compromise. They all encountered Jesus. His word was written on their hearts, they believed it, and Jesus was an ever-present help in time of need to these men who were not willing to compromise.

I will use Daniel because the Lord said something profound to Daniel. *"And He said unto me, O Daniel, a man greatly beloved, understand the words that I speak unto thee am I now sent. And when He had spoken this word unto me, I stood trembling. Then said He unto me, Fear not Daniel: for from the first day that thou didst set thine heart to understand and to chasten thyself before thy God, thy words were heard, and I am come for thy words"* (Daniel 10:11-12). What an honor for Jesus to say, "your prayers were heard and I am come for your words." The Jesus speaking is the One whose eyes are like flames of fire, and His hair is white like wool. This is the Jesus that had John the Revelator on the floor as a dead man. Daniel too was on the floor, standing and trembling. God had him all messed up. A true encounter with God will have you undone, just ask Isaiah. The scriptures go on to say something very interesting concerning what Daniel will be shown. *"But I will show thee that which is noted in the scripture of truth: and there is none that holdeth with me in these things, but Michael your prince"* (Daniel 10:21). Daniel in this chapter has seen a vision of Jesus. Now the Author Himself is revealing the scriptures of truth to Daniel. The word "show" also means to announce, expose, predict, manifest, and explain.

Daniel sees Jesus, and now the scriptures are being explained. What an awesome day for Daniel. Jesus is showing us some of His desires here, and it is Jesus who longs for men to see Him. He also greatly desires men to encounter Him in the scriptures because He Himself is the Author, and not only that, but He is the Word. If you look carefully, Jesus came to His disciples who were going from Emmaus to Jerusalem and spoke to them about Himself in the scriptures. Now to Daniel He comes to him and reveals the scriptures to him. Evidently the scriptures are pretty important to Jesus.

When Jesus was tempted of the devil in the wilderness, the Living Word, Himself, referred to the written word and told Satan, it is written! So the Living Word will absolutely refer to the Written Word, because He is the Author, while men are merely His scribes. The Author and Finisher of our faith desires to speak to us in His word.

The resurrected Jesus opened the scriptures to His disciples and caused their hearts to burn. God has a great purpose in all that He does, and some of the things that He is doing is preparing His people for what is coming. Paul had scripture opened to him, and he in turn opened it to us when he said "that Rock was Christ" (1 Corinthians 10:4). The Old Testament does not say that, but as Jesus opened scripture to him and gave him revelation, He says it and it is in the Bible and is accepted as truth because it is in the Bible. The Bible is true because its Author is Truth; my question is how much truth has the body of Christ corporately not walked into due to a lame spirit. If we are being lead into all truth, it means we are going somewhere, and when we are going somewhere, then signs and wonders should follow us. Then others should taste of the goodness and mercy of our God.

Scripture being opened is the beginning of a journey that God has planned for every believer. Whether the journey takes us to the Nations, to work, to the hospital, or the church office, nevertheless, there is a radical journey of love that the Lamb has in store for those who will walk worthy of Him.

After Jesus was resurrected from the dead, He says something and then expounded all things in the scriptures concerning Himself. Look at what He said first; *"Then He said unto them, O fools, and slow of heart to believe all that the prophets have spoken: Ought not Christ to have suffered these things, and to enter into His glory?"* (Luke 24:25-26). Jesus calls them fools, and then causes their hearts to burn as He opens the scriptures to them. Jesus does not only analyze the problem, He solves it also. It does not take a prophet to tell you bad news, just read the newspapers daily and you will hear plenty of bad news. Jesus "beginning at Moses and all the prophets expounded the things concerning Himself." Then Jesus sits to eat with them, breaks bread and gives it to them. Now we pick up the story again; *"And their eyes were opened, and they knew Him; and He vanished out of their sight. And they said one to another, did not our hearts burn within us, while He talked with us by the way, and while He opened to us the scriptures?"* (Luke 24:31-32). They did not have a debate, they spoke about how their hearts burned. They did not argue, they spoke about their experience with Jesus as He opened the scriptures on the way. Jesus is the way and in Him, He will definitely open the scriptures to His body, He is doing it like never before. People with experience with Jesus love to speak about it, people that lack experience like to debate and accuse others. Jesus miraculously vanished but they did not talk about His miracle, for He had previously done many miracles. One of His names, "Wonderful," literally means miracle. God was doing a new thing, and that was the topic of their conversation. What God is doing should be the topic of our conversations. When what the enemy is doing is the majority of what we speak about, it shows that we are sick. Jesus manifested to destroy the works of the enemy, not talk about them. If the enemy can get us to frequently dwell on and talk about what he is doing, he can neutralize us and cause us to backslide, apostatize, and lose our first love. Our first love will always be our first focus, what we are focused on, we are filled with. Out of the abundance of the heart the mouth speaks.

Jesus just previously took bread, broke it, and supernaturally vanished. He did not eat any bread, for He gave it away. So then in Luke 24:36, He supernaturally appears in the midst of them, they see the pierced Jesus who is risen from the grave. He gives them a brief lesson, that spirits have not flesh and bones, and then He asks His awe struck disciples if they have any meat. So Jesus gave bread, and now He is asking for meat, what is He, a faith preacher? I guess Jesus believes in the hundred-fold return, ha-ha! He then eats in front of them, and fulfills more scripture. It is like you cannot stop Him from doing it.

> *"And He said unto them, These are words which I spake unto you, while I was yet with you, that all things must be fulfilled, which were written in the Law of Moses, and in the prophets, and in the Psalms concerning me. Then He opened their understanding, that they might understand the scriptures"* (Luke 24:44-45).

Jesus tells them the message to preach, tells them they are the witnesses of these things, and then He sends them to Jerusalem and tells them to wait until they are endued with power from on high. The power of God is absolutely necessary for authentic ministry. For an authentic minister, godly character is a must or Jesus is completely miss-represented. Most of the things that are done wrong in the church are because there is little understanding of scripture and hardly any reverence for it. Other church disappointments usually spawn from people not deeply knowing the Author Himself. This leads to the church miss-representing Jesus to the world, which to me is a HUGE SIN, and needs to be repented of. Two different times Jesus had direct involvement with the scriptures after His resurrection. One time He expounded unto them all the scriptures concerning Himself. The word expounded, means to explain thoroughly or to translate. They received the Jesus translation; live from the pierced One, what a time for an altar call. Then Jesus supernaturally vanished and then supernaturally appears in the midst where He belongs. Yet again we see King Jesus opening their understanding of scripture, Jesus seems pretty fervent about this. Then Jesus opened their understanding or intellect that they might understand or put together, act piously and be wise. Jesus tells them to be wise. With the scriptures being opened to them, makes them wise and gives them their sermon and tells them to wait for power, and then they will preach. Even after seeing a resurrected Jesus, who was pierced, He still wanted them to be filled with the Holy Ghost before their first sermon. I wrote about this because it is something the Lord Jesus is doing now in the earth. He is opening the scriptures. Remember Jesus did this before He poured out His Spirit, and even then, Peter was able to say that this is what was written about in the book of Joel. With scripture, He put language to what God was doing. This is important, like when Jesus is doing something His people have never seen before, He will identify it by His voice and also invite you to walk on the water as He and Peter did. There is something God has in store. I know this because of Him opening scripture. Shortly after the scriptures were open to them, the Spirit of God fell upon them in a mighty way. If God does not pour out His Spirit upon us, there is no way we will endure what is shortly coming upon the face of the whole earth. The scriptures being opened is the beginning of something good. What God is doing is so precious to me, I desperately want to not only be where God is moving, but I want to be what He is doing.

Peter was living in the fulfillment of prophecy in Acts 10, when he went into a trance, and Jesus told him to "rise, kill, and eat." This seemed to contradict everything he had been taught; yet at that time he did not know what to do. Jesus was not contradicting the Law, He had fulfilled the Law, and what was once unclean was now clean. This completely contradicted what was written in the Law, but the Law was fulfilled in Jesus Christ and the New Testament had to be written for us to read. This vision became a New Testament doctrine. When Paul said, "food is sanctified by the Word of God and prayer," Jesus wasn't going against scripture. He was just continuing to write it so we could have a Bible that would complete the full counsel of God. The Father desired to give us everything that pertained to life and godliness in a person, in a book and us for us. I wonder how religious Jews took Peter's new revelation; they probably called him a heretic or whatever. So we must have a pure heart, so we can see what God is doing. We also must have clean hands, so we can get them in on what God is doing. This is co-laboring. Another brief example, Joseph, according to the Law, could have stoned Mary who was pregnant with Jesus, but he did not choose to, because he was gracious and kind. The religious world might have called him a compromiser or whatever they said in those days, but he knew the revelation he had received. However, he had no reference point, he just had a pure heart and was a man of character who would trust God and bear the reproach of that. Joseph's decision, to be merciful, got him more time with Jesus than any other human in the days of his flesh. Jesus worked with Joseph for 18 years, from sun up until sun down, six days a week. Look how much time Joseph got to spend with God, when the people who most likely accused him probably did not even believe in Jesus. There are false encounters, which men and women are having with angels and apostles of light. Even the enemy disguises himself and comes like an angel of light. As God opens the scriptures, the enemy will contend with a counterfeit to cause men to stray from Jesus Christ, our Passover Lamb. If the word of God is not revered and Jesus is not the center, it is probably not of God. Jesus Christ is the centrality of all God is doing. This is something you should hear, take heed that no man deceives you. A picture of this would be a man walking up the steps holding the railing using wisdom. Being afraid of deception, you are already deceived. A picture of someone being afraid of being deceived is someone crawling up the stairs with a helmet on, holding on the railing with both hands. The spirit of fear is one of the governors who administrate deception, the enemy is afraid because he is judged. We should only fear God, who judges. We must stay in the word of God and obey what it says. We must be of a humble heart, and stay in fellowship with sincere believers. This is practical advice but remember God began a good work in us and He will finish it, after all, He is the Author and the Finisher. Those who put their trust in Him will never be ashamed. We eat the scroll, and we will know what is God and what is not God. We must keep our eyes on Jesus, because His eyes are on us. We can love Him because He first loved us. When we eat the scroll, the Word will become flesh. When the Word is flesh in us, it is then when our Christianity becomes visible to those around us.

Jesus is the Word that became flesh, and dwelt amongst us. We are in desperate need for Jesus to walk among us in these last days. We cannot afford for Jesus to be knocking on the door of our churches, while hell opens up its mouth and swallows my generation. The Word must become flesh in us, so others can touch Jesus as we walk through the everyday normal life. Jesus must be tangible, not just at a Gospel crusade but also in you and me everyday. When the Word is flesh in us, Jesus is tangible. He is not some kind of a philosophy that we can debate over. Instead of debating about Jesus and Paul's Epistles, we should try manifesting Him to a lost and dying world. Manifesting Jesus, when the word is not flesh in us, is a delusion of grandeur to even think about. The enemy comes to steal the seed of the Word, so it does not become flesh, and replicate what Jesus did and destroy the destroyer's works.

The mystery of godliness deals with the Word becoming flesh. *"And without controversy great is the mystery of godliness: God was manifested in the flesh, justified in the Spirit, seen of angels, preached unto the Gentiles, believed on in the world, received up into glory"* (1 Timothy 3:16). This is the six-fold mystery of godliness. We are going to touch the issue of the Word becoming flesh, because it is the beginning of the progression of this beautiful mystery. Jesus was born of a virgin, the Holy Spirit overshadowed Mary, and she became impregnated with God who was going to be manifested in the flesh. Jesus was fully God and fully man. He was fully God so He manifested in the flesh. He was also born of a virgin, therefore He was fully man. I believe it was the Spirit of Life, which over shadowed Mary and brought life where there was none. The Spirit of Life is mentioned in Revelation 11:11, and also in Romans 8:2&10; check those verses out.

A great picture of the mystery of godliness is seen in the book of Ezekiel. God commands Ezekiel to speak His words, but first something happens. Let's read it together. This marvelous encounter Ezekiel has with the Lord is awesome, it is found in the second chapter of Ezekiel. Here is a little background information on the first chapter of Ezekiel. The throne of God was pursuing Ezekiel, and he wound up face down, all messed up like anyone who really encounters Jesus. So Ezekiel is down, and Jesus says to him "Son of man stand upon thy feet, and I will speak unto thee." The scripture goes on, "And the Spirit entered into me when He spake unto me, and set me upon my feet." The words of God are Spirit and life, and the Spirit entered him with no invitation. Jesus knocked Paul off his horse without his permission. Religion has taught us some interesting things, like God is a gentlemen and He does not invade free will. Did Ezekiel ask to be picked up by his hair? Did Jonah ask to be put in a whale's belly for three days? The Spirit of God is now in the prophet. Did the Spirit of God live in the Old Testament prophets? I have heard several pastors say that the Spirit of God did not dwell in the Old Testament people, and that is not biblical. It is interesting how Nebuchadnezzar could recognize the Son of God in the fire, in Daniel chapter three, but the Pharisees could not see Him when He was right in front of them. It is similar to pastors clearly contradicting the Bible and people believing it. Religion has taught us stuff that sounds good, but just isn't true. God is bigger than Jonah's free will or Paul's. For God is sovereign. We need to be sure that the Holy Spirit is teaching us God's word, not men giving us their opinions of God's word. Men's opinions lead to heresy; while God's opinion and perspective is called the truth. When the Word becomes flesh, the truth becomes visible. That is the will of God, on earth as it is in heaven. What is invisible becomes visible when we are with God for the impossible.

Ezekiel sees the throne pursing him which puts Ezekiel on his face. Jesus' words are so powerful they literally put a prostrate man on his feet. Did Ezekiel ask to be stood up? Did Ezekiel ask to have the Holy Spirit come in? You can settle this between you and Jesus, but while Jesus or the Word of the Lord is commissioning Ezekiel, we see a picture in scripture of a mystery.

> *"But thou, son of man, hear what I say unto thee; Be not thou rebellious like that rebellious house: open thy mouth, and eat that I give thee, And when I looked, behold a hand was sent unto me; and, lo, a roll of a book was therein; And He spread it before me; and it was written within and without: and there was written therein lamentations, and mourning, and woe. Moreover He said unto me, Son of man, eat that thou findest; eat this roll, and go speak unto the house of Israel. So I opened my mouth, and He caused me to eat the roll. And He said unto me, Son of man, cause thy belly to eat, and fill thy bowels with this roll that I give thee. Then did I eat it; and it was in my mouth as honey for sweetness. And He said unto me, Son of man, go get thee unto the house of Israel, and speak with my words unto them"* (Ezekiel 2:8, 3:4).

When John the Revelator in Revelation ten ate the scroll, the results were the same; bitter and sweet. This is the tension of the word. What is interesting about what the Lord did with Ezekiel is

He gave him the scroll and told him to eat and go. He did not say eat, wait, fast, and pray. There is a time for every purpose under heaven, but fasting and praying does not negate our commission to go into the entire world and preach. Jesus' hand did not feed Ezekiel the scroll so Ezekiel could be spiritual, but so the people of God could hear the word of God. The Word had to live in Ezekiel before he could speak it, or he would be a hypocrite. Ezekiel ate the scroll as the Lord had told him to do, and then went where the Lord told him to go. There is no way you could have eaten the scroll, and then not go where you are being sent. Jonah did not even eat a scroll, he just ran from God's voice and wound up in a whale. God is so serious about His redemptive purposes, that He will put someone in a whale and spit him out to accomplish what is in His heart for lost humanity.

"Go" is in the word God. "Go" is also in the word good news. "Go" is in the word gospel. If you have really eaten and tasted, you will go and proclaim. There is no way you can spend time with the real Jesus and not tell people about Him. When someone gets married, they naturally tell everyone and it is just like this when someone really knows Jesus. It is natural, not a choice or an event, but a privilege and honor. The problem is most Christians do not understand that a blood covenant does not have much to do with feelings, but has a lot to do with commitment that is greater than a feeling. Preaching the gospel is part of our love for Jesus. Jesus Himself said, "If you love me, obey me." Jesus said to love the Lord your God, and love your neighbor as yourself. He also said to come and learn from Me, for I am gentle and lowly in heart, and He said go and preach! It is impossible to have eaten the scroll, and not to have told people about Him. It is delusional to even think that Jesus can touch us, and we can remain the same. Can we touch a burning hot frying pan and be the same? Well our God is a consuming fire, so if the way really touches us, can we continue to be lost? If we have really eaten the scroll, we will have to do things His way. The Word must be flesh before God sends us. Man will send the educated, but God sends only dedicated. The word becoming flesh is one of the requirements of being sent by God, man can send anyone.

Those who God sends are not moved by how they are received. Noah preached for over 100 years with no converts, just his family was saved. They were not even going to listen to Ezekiel, and God told him that before He sent him. Sometimes it is not about them listening, but about us listening. God would take His time and talk to Ezekiel about people who were not even going to listen to him. That is an all-wise God. The word must become flesh if we are not going to be moved by the world around us. When the Word is flesh in us we will not be moved by the world around us, but will be moved by the Spirit in us. Jesus, who was the Word Himself who became flesh, was tangible to the outside world. The woman with the issue of blood touched Him and was never the same, and her issue of blood dried up immediately. As the Word becomes flesh in us and we are sent, others must be able to touch the Christ in us, which is the hope of glory. You and I might be the only hope someone ever has to touch Jesus. Therefore we must eat the scroll, or others will starve. His word must be living in us like an active volcano that reacts when the fault line shifts. Most Christians are dormant volcanoes that religion, disappointment, and rejection have silenced. The shaking that is coming hopefully will shift the fault lines and cause an eruption of what is within to come out. It is very hard to have a burden for the lost, when you yourself are lost. Where can a lost person go or be sent? If we are not hearing Jesus and obeying Him, perhaps we can go to church for twenty years and be as lost as a hooker on the street corner.

Those in whom the Word truly does become flesh, suffer

persecution. You can only live godly in Christ Jesus, if you abide in Him and His words abide in you. When the word of God offends you, there is a breach in the life and the Spirit of God, because light only offends darkness. Which is why they have nothing in common, and do not fellowship together. The Spirit of God, the Word of God, and the people of God are the keys to living godly in Christ Jesus. No amount of scripture reading or praying subsidizes for the mystery of our fellowship, and the relationships we are called to have being knit together in love. No amount of fasting and praying fulfills our holy obligation to preach the gospel. Also no amount of preaching fulfills our bridal privilege of fasting and praying and being intimate with Jesus. They are all necessary. When the Word has become flesh and is living in us, we become whole Christians. Meaning we pray, we preach, we fast, we give, we become willing to go, we go, we lay down our lives, we have joy in abasing, and we have joy in abounding. The full counsel of God's word is very much needed in this hour, like never before. People camp out around one realm of truth, and become proud and delusional to think we do not need one another. This is a disease. It is called spiritual pride and it got Satan thrown out of heaven, and it makes the earth want to vomit its inhabitants.

The bride makes herself ready, because the Groom lives in her and she begins to perceive His desires. As the Word becomes flesh, she becomes ready.

Part of the six-fold mystery of godliness is also the resurrection of the Lord Jesus, but before He could be resurrected, He had to offer His life. Before we can offer our lives, the Word must become flesh in us, and then people are able to touch Jesus or the Christ in us. Then persecution arises because of the Words sake. It is then when we will have the privilege of offering our life, for the One who ransomed Himself for us.

The mystery of godliness, further in the progression of the six-fold mystery is seen also in the book of Ezekiel. Jesus is always right there concerning this mystery.

Christ Jesus must be the center of anything that is truly of God. Most Christians are very familiar with the story of the Valley of Dry Bones. The hand of the Lord carried me out in the spirit of the Lord, so the hand of God comes upon Ezekiel and carries him away. You will either get carried away by God and with Him, or fall away from Him. So then this encounter is similar to John being in the Spirit on the Lord's Day. These men are being wholly possessed by God. Then the Lord starts asking Ezekiel some questions, and Ezekiel said, "Lord, you know." Then Jesus said, "Prophesy to these bones." So Ezekiel did as he was commanded to do; *"So I was commanded: and as I prophesied, there was a noise, and behold a shaking, and the bones came together, bone to his bone. And when I beheld, lo, the sinews and the flesh came upon them, and skin covered them above: but there was no breath in them"* (Ezekiel 37:7-8). The Word became flesh in the disciples, then the wind of God blew upon them in the Upper Room, and then they had to take it out. They did not stay in the Upper Room; they brought their Upper Room experience out. It brought them into the same Sanhedrin that condemned Jesus to die, but their experience took the fear out of them. Their experience of the wind of God brought them to prison, and some to exile, and some to their own crosses. If you were to ask them, "is it worth it?" they would smile at you and say yes! Before the wind came into the dry bones, the prophetic word that the Lord commanded shifted the structure of the bones, they moved and then the Word became flesh. This is what is happening even now. The Lord is shifting the structure of His church, by turning the hearts of fathers to their children. Prophecy is being fulfilled even now. Some of the church is falling away, and in the midst of that, a bride is making herself ready, as she prepares to meet her Bridegroom.

Back to Ezekiel; the Lord tells Ezekiel to prophesy to the wind and he does, and life comes into what was dead and dry. So you had a valley of death and disunity. A "valley of dry bones" should be the name of some churches. This is where we are really at, similar to Hannah. She knew her husband, but she was barren. We somewhat know Jesus, but are yet to prove it to the world around us. God must hear our cry of barrenness, and the expression of the womb must be committed to Him if a true prophetic generation will come forth. If Charles Finney or Andrew Murray or Watchman Nee saw the people we call prophets, they would call them comedians. So before the Word became flesh in the valley of dry bones, there had to be a shift and a shaking of the bones that were dead. Prophetically this is where I believe we are. Then after the word was prophesied, the Word became flesh and life is now a possibility. After the shifting and shaking, the bones become unified to be alive. This begins to happen as God begins to corporately speak to His people. I believe this is where the forerunners of this generation currently are. Then Ezekiel prophesies to the wind, and life comes into the bones which were once dead. Now they have become an exceeding great army. Scripture goes on to say that this is the house of Israel and they are people of Covenant. If we are Christians, we are also people of covenant. If God made a second and better covenant with us, how greatly do you think the Holy Spirit wants to blow a wind on the people of God? Ezekiel is safely prophesying, because he is real close to Jesus and the timing of his prophecy is right after he was commanded. Ezekiel is speaking God's word, right next to God, in His timing. This is a lesson on how to safely prophesy. Before prophesying, the Word must be flesh in you. No one would want to hear Jesus say to them, "depart from me, I don't know you, you worker of iniquity."

Yet Jesus, I prophesied in your name? So did the women with

90

the spirit of divination in the book of Acts, and she prophesied 100 percent accurately, but the devil lived in her. God used Paul to free her up, which put him behind bars. The issue is the Word becoming flesh and manifesting the mystery of godliness. All who live godly will become content, for godliness with contentment is great gain. The mystery of godliness is the Word becoming flesh. When the Word becomes flesh in us, we live godly, this provokes persecution and also great blessing. Contentment is wrapped up in the truth that Jesus will never leave us nor forsake us. So when persecution arises for the Word's sake, the Word Himself will not leave us and we realize that we have gained the only thing that is really worth anything anyway. We have gained Jesus. Paul did not mind losing to truly gain, he even said to die is gain. Gain is not what we can get, but how much we can give. Giving our life for Jesus is the greatest gain possible. The grace of biblical gain is awesome, because it is not about us but about Jesus. May we learn to gain Jesus, and give an accurate witness to those around us of who He is and what He is really like.

The dry bones becoming flesh is a type of resurrection from the dead, and it is also a part of the six fold mystery of godliness. Godliness ushers in persecution; persecution allows us to see if our roots are in Christ, and if we have built our house upon the Rock. Our house is a wellspring of life also; there is no one like our Jesus. Like physical houses have a hose spigot, our house has the water of life that flows from it also.

In the parable of the Seed and the Sower, the context is not a big church with a big preacher and the seed is not your money. The Sower is the Son of God, the seed is the life of His Word, and the thief is the enemy himself. We see in the story of Job that the enemy attacks health, wealth, and family to really try to get Job to compromise the word and curse God, because God has cursed the enemy. So Satan is trying to make Job partake of his very life, by stealing God's word. He was unsuccessful; Job was restored to seven times what he had previously possessed. Even his daughters wound up with an inheritance, which was abnormal in those times.

If we ever read the Bible, Jesus wins! Jesus describes our adversary, the devil.

> *"The thief cometh not, but to steal, and to kill, and to destroy. I am come that they might have life, and that they might have it more abundantly"* (John 10:10).

Lack and sickness are from the devil; poverty and disease are sin's 401 k plan with eternal fire. Jesus is abundant in every way. That is why the increase of His government and peace, shall be no end. Jesus is eternally abundant in what He does, but He never has to change. He is more than amazing; He is God in the flesh. He does exceedingly abundantly more than we can ask or think according to the power that works in us. Jesus through His disciple's obedience brought about lunch for thousands of people and His disciples each receiving an extra basket of food to take home. That was like supernatural take out food! We must be filled with the Holy Spirit; again abundance seems normal to God. We are only as filled as much as you overflow onto others. The thief, who comes to steal the word, has tactics and they are not new. A familiar spirit that is familiar with your behavior can come to you in an unfamiliar way. However, the enemy does not have any new tactics.

Jesus would not tell us the parable of the seed and the sower, and not tell us in scripture how to position ourselves not to be a victim of robbery. Robbing God in the tithe is a way that the enemy has access into our lives. There are many things a believer does ignorantly that gives the thief legal access, if we spoke about that, this would turn into an encyclopedia. However, we are talking about positioning and also proximity. I learned the word "proximity" from a Pastor in Pennsylvania, and it never left me.

This issue is seen clearly in the story of Mary and Martha. Mary sits at Jesus' feet, and Martha is serving people, and was encumbered or busy with much serving. Martha had a burden to accuse Mary, but Mary had a burden to hear Jesus. Jesus rebuked Martha. The issue is not that Mary did not have a servant's heart, but she was more interested in God than serving hot food. Those with a works mentality have a tendency to accuse others. Many people use this Mary and Martha story to get out of fulfilling their obligation to serve others, for the Son of Man came not to be served but to serve. The issue is the timing, when Jesus is speaking it is not a time to be serving but a time to be listening and paying close attention.

"And Jesus answered and said unto her, Martha, Martha, thou art careful

and troubled about many things: But one thing is needful: and Mary hath chosen that good part, which shall not be taken from her" (Luke 10:41-42). The wood, hay, and stubble will all be burned away. Martha was actually deceived by thinking that what she was doing was right, when she was really wrong. Someone who is deceived tends to be an accuser also, the devil is the deceiver and the accuser, and so they go together. You can tell that this is Martha's soul, not a demonic spirit, because if it were a demon spirit Jesus would have addressed it. Jesus knows everything you know. Martha is living her Christian life here in the flesh and Jesus rebukes her. In the realm of proximity or nearness to Jesus, Mary is closer because she is at His feet. She is low by His feet, so she is positioned at a low place. This speaks of true humility. Perhaps a great picture of false humility is being busy serving God, but giving no attention to His voice.

Mary's not rebuking Martha because her eyes are fixed on the One she loves. Mary is a picture of first love; Martha is a picture of a loss of first love, or one who never had it to begin with. When Jesus says, "one thing is needful;" needful literally means business, requirement, and employment necessary. Mary was just doing her job, minding her own business. She was sitting at His feet, hearing His word. Martha, however, was doing something noble. She was preparing food for the people of God, which is quite a noble thing. Yet Mary was already eating while Martha was busy preparing food. Jesus said something interesting, it is this; "Mary has chosen which shall not be taken away from her." This is a huge statement, one of the boldest statements in the Bible. When Jesus is referring to what will not be taken from her, He is speaking of His word. She has positioned herself in a way that, we should take note of and learn from. She in proximity is very close and near to the Lord Jesus, she in vision is fully focused. Mary says nothing against her accuser. She does not defend herself because she knows her advocate. Her position is low at His feet, which reflects her humility. Mary's priorities are right and this will bring about the right results. The richest King employs her. She will never be laid off or unemployed. When Jesus says that she has chosen the good part that shall not be taken from her, He means it. The Word was received and it will bear fruit. In my honest opinion, it seems she will bear 100 fold fruit, because of the seed's exposure to the Son! There is a specific group of people in the scriptures that find themselves at Jesus' feet. Some of them are Daniel, Ezekiel, and John the Revelator. And there was Mary, the women who anointed Jesus' feet, whose story is told where ever the gospel is preached for a memorial to her. I am particularly fond of people who find themselves at Jesus' feet. My absolute favorite thing to do is spend time with Jesus. The place of light or revelation is at Jesus' feet. Someone who has revelation must be singly focused on Jesus alone. These are the people Jesus can trust, these are those who steward the mysteries of God, these are the people who others want to accuse. The devil hates these people, because he cannot steal from them, and they will willingly give their lives, which he cannot destroy. John the Revelator had a burden to lay his head on Jesus' chest. John wanted to be near to Jesus, and John also showed up at the cross. He out ran Peter to the grave, outlived all the disciples, and received the Revelation of Jesus Christ in exile. Daniel had so much prophetic revelation, God told him to close the book for it was for a later time. Daniel also wound up at the feet of Jesus. In the book of Revelation there is something interesting concerning the position of being at the feet of Jesus that forever changed my life. It gave me understanding as to why, I did something specific without really knowing why I did it. *"And when I saw Him, I fell at His feet as dead. And He laid His right hand upon me, saying unto me, Fear not; I am the first and the last"* (Revelation 1:17). In that verse the word "fell" literally means to fall lightly on. It was after falling face down that He then received the Revelation for the seven churches. The Lord Jesus could trust John with His bride due to his commitment to Him personally. John saw Him and fell down. The woman with the alabaster box broke it and poured it out on Him because she perceived who He really was and what was soon to be in store for Him. Mary sat at His feet. I wonder, did Martha really see Jesus? I believe if her spirit saw Jesus, she too would have been at His feet. Do we really see Jesus?

I never like to be robbed, nobody really does, so why would they bother to attain what they are going to get if they are going to rob anyway. The fact that the Holy Scriptures teach us how not to be robbed, really should give us great joy. It is true that God is really good; it is not just a church people slogan. I say that joking but I have heard many teachings, and people's perspective of God is horrible. This shows me that they have been robbed, and offended. If we are offended, it is probably an indication that we need to repent, and change the way we think, once and for all.

Jesus' earthy mother Mary pondered the Word of God in her heart, this gave the seed time to grow. This is also very wise to do. We are told to meditate in the law, day and night, so that we pre-meditate righteousness. The heart must be good ground, for the seed to grow. The seed also grows with the watering of the Holy Spirit and direct contact with Son light. Mary not only was hearing the word of God, she was also in the presence of God. Most of the problem in the here and now is that we hear the word of God with very little presence. Our hearts are filled with other things, and we do not take time to ponder the word. We need the presence of God, that is why Mary would not be robbed, and what she has chosen could not be taken from her. She was hearing the word in the presence of God. Jesus never spoke or heard the word of God outside the presence of God. We should really learn from Him, He does know everything! If we learn from Him, He will teach us to do greater works than even He did. Yet a servant is not greater than his master. Jesus is the humblest person I know, and I do not think there is anywhere better to be than at His feet. Wise virgins know where to get oil; they also know who to spend the oil on. Staying at the feet of Jesus will keep you humble and teach you how to tremble. The biggest thing I will promote is for people to spend one on one time with Jesus. A husband and a wife do not make children in public, but in private. Your fruitfulness comes when you adhere to your Bridegroom's desire. The desire is this; *"Rise up, my love, my fair one, and come away"* (Song of Solomon 2:10&13). In order to become bold and rise up, we must come away with Him. It is His voice that draws us deeper into His presence.

"Now when they saw the boldness of Peter and John, and perceived that they were ignorant men they marveled; and they took knowledge of them, that they had been with Jesus" (Acts 4:13). It was not their eloquence or their skills to debate, but their boldness that allowed the religious world to know they were with Jesus. Since they knew, that is what Jesus produced. When the Romans came to get Jesus, He stepped forward, and they fell back and Jesus said, I am He who you seek. Many people need to just spend time with Jesus and stop running from the One who is seeking them. Jesus will make us bold naturally; we do not have to wait in an impartation line. That is good, but the best thing you can do for yourself is deny yourself and pursue time with the One who can redeem time. I believe in impartation and healing, but I know that wise virgins do not try to buy oil from the other virgins. The lesson I see in that is that man is not your source. If you are a wise virgin, you will join the other four wise virgins who went out to meet the Bridegroom, and wind up at the foot of His cross. Remember five people showed up at the foot of the cross of Jesus. We have oil in our lamps so that our light can shine in the darkness.

When darkness covered the face of the entire world during the crucifixion of Jesus, five wise virgins let their light shine before men as they went out to meet the Bridegroom.

The Word of God is sown on the soil of men's hearts. That is why the Prophet Hosea said to *"Sow to yourselves in righteousness, reap in mercy; break up the fallow ground: for it is time to seek the Lord, till He come and rain righteousness upon you"* (Hosea 10:12). Jesus is righteousness rained down on us. Most people have a very hard time hearing the voice of God because they have not and do not know how to break up the fallow ground. The Prophet Jeremiah also had something to say about this issue of fallow ground, because it contains something that chokes the seed. *"For thus saith the Lord to the men of Judah and Jerusalem, Break up your fallow ground, and sow not among thorns. Circumcise yourselves to the Lord, and take away the foreskins of your heart, ye men of Judah and inhabitants of Jerusalem: lest my fury come forth like fire, and burn that none can quench it, because of the evil of your doings"* (Jeremiah 4:3-4). Jeremiah is speaking of their hearts as the fallow ground that needs to be broken up, not only that, but he is saying their hearts are unclean with thorns in them. Many people analyze the deep problems of the church, and it all really boils down to the hearts of men. If our heart is right, the seed of the Word grows in us. As it grows, Christ is formed in us, this gives us a broken and contrite heart and spirit. A broken and contrite heart is a heart that hears and feels. A heart that truly hears will listen and obey. In the parable of the Seed and the Sower, when the Word is sown it is a person, not a scripture or theological theory. It's Christ Jesus Himself. The progression of the growth of the seed is the Word finding good ground and growing in us. This is none other than "Christ in you, the hope of glory." The Word receives the rain of the Holy Spirit and growth takes place. Before any growth can take place, the seed must be sown in to the earth and the shell of the seed must be broken. The life of the seed goes into the soil and then rain and sunlight cause growth. Over time we have the fruit of whatever seed that has been sown. The Sower and the Seed are one because He sowed His very own life. The seed is not just some great sermon. Many men could preach great sermons, but only Jesus is worthy to ransom His life and divine nature that we might receive Him and be partakers of His divine nature. Many Christians talk about finding their purpose, but they are lost. How can a lost person find their purpose? Their real purpose is to lose their lives so that they find their life. Jesus is life. Knowing Him and making Him known is the simplicity of Christ. It is all about Him. When the Word opened the scriptures to the disciples, they found out it was really all about Jesus. It was then that He could trust them with the real power, which caused them not to love their lives. Before the seed is sown the fallow ground must be broken up, and the thorns must be taken out, and a circumcision of the heart must take place by the word of God that divides the soul from the spirit. Thorns are definitely not wanted in your heart. Jesus was violently pierced on His head with thorns, and He definitely does not want them in your heart choking out His very life in you. Jesus' life paid sin's penalty. The wages of sin is death, so Jesus gave His life. The blood of Christ paid for us. Our gift of salvation was free, but it cost God His Son. His name is the Word of God. Jesus broke the power of sin, which means we should not be under it. He broke the power of death, so why should we fear it? He has eternal stripes for temporary healing, why be sick? There are unsearchable riches in Christ Jesus, why live in poverty? When the Nations are in derision the Lord sits in the heavens and laughs, why be depressed? We the church, by and large, have not deeply understood the depth of the sacrifice of the Lord Jesus. So, we could only be trusted with very little of the riches of His Word and how it applies to us in every area of our lives. The more we are faithful, the more God will entrust to us; this was seen very clearly in Jesus' parable of the Talents.

The word must be guarded because the word also guards us from being partakers of what Jesus has ransomed us from. The wages of sin is death, sin is expensive and a horrible investment. In America they will slaughter your child at an abortion slaughterhouse for under $1,000. There are probably some people who have acquired credit card debt from killing multiple babies. Drugs will also drain your pocket. Materialism will leave you in major debt. Sin is expensive, Jesus paid a high price for us and we must guard our hearts. When a heart is guarded it is filled with the Word.

The Word of God is sown on the soil of our hearts, the Psalmist said; *"thy word have I hid in my heart that I might not sin against thee"* (Psalm 119:11). The payment for sin was the Word who became flesh; the One who keeps us from sin, is the Word who lives in us. Solomon said, *"Keep thy heart with all diligence; for out of it flow the issues of life"* (Proverbs 4:23).

The heart is something that constantly must be kept, and guarded. In the New Testament there is actually a breastplate of righteousness that protects it. Righteousness is only attained through the blood of the Lamb, the blood that makes us righteous. The act that made us righteous also protects His very life in us.

The heart is so delicate, that the Lord just gives us a new one instead of repairing the old one. I have heard many Christians say that "the heart is deceitfully wicked, who can know it." Jesus was fully aware of that, that is why in the New Covenant, He promised a new heart according to Ezekiel 36:26; *"A new heart also will I give you, and a new spirit will I put within you: and I will take away your stony heart out of your flesh, and I will give you an heart of flesh."* This certainly is not a deceitfully wicked heart. The new heart sometimes can be broken, so He will bind it up. Other times it becomes a little dirty, He then sanctifies it. The Lord Jesus expects our participation and our participation is called discipleship. It is all about Him, He pretty much does it all, but we must be the gatekeepers of what He has given to us. We decide who and what we allow into, what God has given us. We learn from Jesus that defilement is from within. Judas betrayed Jesus from within his own ministry. If you want to see how defiled people are, just listen to them speak. I have heard Christians speak worse of each other than angels speak about the devil. I have even wept over my participation in this foolish behavior. The book of Hebrews contains great illustrations of defilement. *"Looking diligently lest any man fail of the grace of God; lest any root of bitterness springing up trouble you, and there by many be defiled"* (Hebrews 12:15). We the Church talk about each other, about sinners, and about leaders of our nation. It is funny how Jesus never spoke evil of Caesar, but why? Because Jesus appointed him, why would Jesus speak evil of whom He appointed? All authority comes from God, because He created all things. So if He really wants to dethrone someone, He will. He did it in Acts chapter twelve, when the Angel of the Lord executed capital punishment on Herod in front of a crowd of people. (see Acts 12:2-24) Look how Daniel spoke to a king who tried to make him bow his knee to idolatry. Daniel spoke to a heathen king with honor and called him "your majesty," yet he did not bow to him. He adhered to God's law and did not compromise what God said to say or do, but he spoke with honor. The way Daniel spoke may have caused a king to fast and pray that God would save Daniel from a law that he had made. He did not speak evil of the king who was evil. Speaking evil of someone who is already evil does not help that person, prayer does. Also a proper representation of who Jesus really is.

A double-hearted man will be unfaithful nine out of ten times. It is crucial that we break up the fallow ground of our hearts lest they fail or faint in the day of adversity. The tension that is coming to the whole earth shortly, shall cause men's hearts to fail if they are not right with God. According to my understanding, we are in the "beginning of sorrows" as Jesus referenced in Matthew 24:8. This time is to break our hearts so they do not fail in the next season, the days of Noah or the end. The beginning of sorrows is to prepare us for the days of Noah and the return of the Lord Jesus. How our hearts are guarded in this season will determine our eternal stay. We must heed to Solomon's words and diligently keep both life and the knowledge of God flowing from our hearts. If not, then issues, offenses and defilement will flow from defiled hearts. Our hearts are filled by what we see and listen to. Jesus was chastised for our peace; the peace of God that Jesus freely gives, guards our hearts and minds through Christ Jesus. The price He paid for us to have the free gift of His peace is stunning. He was chastised and tortured for His life to be protected in us. He died to live in us, and He lives to pray for us. Jesus gives us gifts, so we can represent His loving nature to those around us. Our hearts must stay tender, so that we can forgive and be forgiven. A tender heart is one that is not offended; it is a burning heart that the Word of God Himself lives in. If you are not telling people about Jesus, it is probably because He does not live in you, or the thorns are choking Him. Jesus suffers the hit for all our bad choices, like Moses getting angry with the people and then he hits the Rock. Paul told us that, that Rock was Christ. *"And did all drink the same spiritual drink: for they drank of that spiritual Rock that followed them: and that Rock was Christ"* (1 Corinthians 10:4). The people drink and Christ gets hit. Jesus has already paid for all of our bad choices, however, there is no need to keep making more. The Word that we guard also guards us and keeps us from sin. The Word that we study, also studies us. Also, the Word that we are to rightly divide also divides us. The Word that protects you from sin, also guides us in the way of everlasting life. Refuse to be offended, forgive and stay in the Word. Jesus said, "If you love me you will keep my word." In order for the word to be kept it must be received, nurtured, and guarded. We must continually be washed and sanctified keeping it tender, so that we can receive from God and forgive others. Our heart is also the Author's drawing board, and He will only paint on something that is clean. A clean heart is the only heart that has access to His presence. *"Who shall ascend into the hill of the Lord? Or who shall stand in His holy place? He that hath clean hands, and a pure heart; who hath not lifted up his soul unto vanity, nor sworn deceitfully"* (Psalm 24:3-4). The presence of the Lord is where everything changes, it is where there is joy unspeakable, and where we are strong, it is the place real believers' flesh even longs to be.

Religion always tries to disqualify us, Satan always is waiting to accuse us, and Jesus is our Advocate who forever lives to make intercession for us. The thing that we think disqualifies us, actually qualifies us. Not many mighty men are chosen, God uses the foolish things in this world to confound the wise, or those who have deceived themselves by the pride of their own heart.

The Holy Bible consists of 66 books, at least 20 of those 66 books were written by murderers. Moses who murdered an Egyptian wrote the first five books. David who wrote most of Psalms was a murderer and adulterer. A murderer that was once Saul, who became Paul by the will of God, wrote 14 out of 27 of the New Testament books. Paul was not only a murderer, for he murdered an innocent young preacher boy while he was preaching God's word. He was responsible for Stephen's death by stoning. Paul was similar to a terrorist or even an abortionist, in the fact that he was shedding innocent blood. Those babies have done nothing wrong, similar to Stephen. Also Solomon, who was a heavy drinker, and a womanizer, wrote three books of the Bible. Matthew was a publican prior to his conversion; a publican was a tax collector. They were known for extracting or taking above and beyond the tax that was due. So you have a guy who once used to take too much from God's people, and now is being used to give them the only thing that is really worth anything anyway, the Gospel. Also Peter, the chosen leader of Jesus' movement, would have had federal charges today if he would have cut off a soldier's ear. The point is we are not disqualified. God still wants to use us, but He really wants us to know Him first. God is self-existent and does not need anyone, but He chose us out of love and desire, not out of need. God does not have needs; He is self sufficient and self-existent. Yet He chose to love us so we could have the benefit of Him, not because He could not do it without us. Only God, because of His unfailing love, can take sinful, fallible, imperfect sinners and make a book that's infallible. With imperfect people, people who fall short, people who have needs and lacks, He can give us a book that has everything that pertains to life in godliness in it. These men were not always inspired by God, much of the time they were inspired by their own flesh, anger, lust, and greed. Yet all scripture is inspired and God breathed by men who were definitely not always inspired by God. Who is like our God, who can make 100 percent success with 100 percent failures?

God used Jonah and Jonah did not even want to be used by God. Jonah wanted God to judge the people and God wanted to save them and send a revival to Nineveh. I do not believe prayer is the key to revival, or America would be in revival. I know people who pray for a living. Jonah did not pray for revival, if anything, he prayed against it. God is the key to revival. I am not minimizing prayer of the believers. I am simply saying God is in charge. If prayer was the key to revival, then Nineveh would have really been out of luck, because the prophet who is supposed to intercede is disappointed at the repentance and the revival that took place. I know many people who would go in the belly of a whale for three days for a revival, let alone run from one. I have no idea why Jonah did not want a revival gathering. Jesus wept over Jerusalem because He wanted to gather them like a mother hen gathers chicks, but they would not. In a move of God, people get healthy, some get wealthy, the lost become found, and persecution arises. Most of all, Jesus is welcome in His church once again. I just do not understand Jonah. However, God does not care if I understand Jonah, He chose to use him and that is the end of the story. God has chosen to use you! Will you participate?

The people God uses to take His Word and bring the Fire of God to a city will baffle you. How about Elijah, he calls fire down from heaven, slays tons of false prophets and then runs from the woman Jezebel. Then Jesus still has him on the mount of Transfiguration, as a special guest with Moses. The Law came through Moses. He was already a murderer as he was writing the Law with his very own hands the second time. The same anger issue that caused him to kill an Egyptian caused him to throw the Law down after he had been with God for 40 days in His manifest glory presence. God wanted to destroy the children of Israel and make Moses a great nation, but Moses had a burden to stand in the gap for the people. God valued this murderer's opinion enough to not wipe out Israel. Look how good God truly is. His goodness in wanting to save people, who did not deserve it, it literally offended Jonah.

God, who is from everlasting to everlasting, inhabits all of eternity. Heaven is His throne and earth is His footstool. He dwells in an unapproachable light, yet tells us in His Holy Word to boldly approach His throne of grace. The throne He sits on has a foundation and it is righteousness and justice. The seat is mercy and the throne is grace. The One who sits on it alone is Holy. God's ways are higher than our ways. They are past finding out, yet His desire is for us to walk in them. This unfailing God uses weakness and failure and foolishness like they are college degrees. Just look at the men He hired in the Bible. This everlasting God uses finite men to bring forth His infallible word. God who is unfailing and perfect uses imperfect men, and through that comes forth the infallible Holy Scriptures - do the math. How does something holy come from someone holy, to mortal men who needed a Savior? You then have an infallible book called the Bible. This really fascinates my heart, thinking of how God perfectly executes His will through very imperfect creatures such as these Bible characters and even you and me. All things that pertain to life and godliness are given through the knowledge of the Son of God, Jesus the Christ. The scriptures, in and of themselves cannot save us, or every person that went into a hotel room in America would be saved - thank you Lord for the Gideons. The same way men in and of themselves could not have written the scriptures; in the same way men cannot understand them, because an unredeemed man is of another spirit. It is as simple as a Chinese person speaking Chinese to someone who only speaks English with no interpreter, without divine assistance it is just not happening. I wish a Scribe or a Pharisee would have been whacked by the Holy Ghost. Oh wait Paul did, and look how effective he was. The law and the prophets were imprinted in Paul's heart; it is clear in his epistles to the churches. I believe a great amount of Paul's fruitfulness in ministry had to do with the will of God, the power of God, and that the Word of God, or the Law of God was opened to him. The Word became flesh causing Him to offer His flesh for the advancement of the Gospel.

From Saul the murderer to Paul the Martyr, a lot happens when the word is open and the Holy Spirit is given to us. Paul the Apostle puts language concerning scripture, being opened from the Old Testament. Philip convinced the Eunuch from Ethiopia with the book of Isaiah, concerning who Jesus really was.

The moral of the story is that our past failures do not disqualify us! His mercy is new every morning. The Son of God wants to impregnate us with the seed of His very own life; He wants to use us to bring forth His word to those who have not heard.

The Gospel must be preached, and we have been nominated, consecrated, commissioned, and commanded. It is not a choice, it is an honor! The fact that He will use us should keep us very grateful, truly humble, and sincere without offense until the day of Christ Jesus.

I am in no way promoting sin, or giving you a license to sin. I am simply saying, if we are willing to come to the Lord, He is willing to change and transform us and conform us into His image. Grace is not cheap; it cost Jesus His life so that He could freely give it to us. The price is so high we should truly cherish it and turn from our sin once and for all. *"Brethren, I count not myself to have apprehended: but this one thing I do, forgetting those things which are behind, and reaching forth unto those things which are before, I press toward the mark for the prize of the high calling of God Christ Jesus"* (Philippians 3:13-14). I simply agree with Paul. Leave the past behind and press into Jesus.

Jesus is soon headed to Calvary in John 17. He will be exposed and nailed to a tree, but He prayed a prayer that is a great privilege to even be able to read first. In the prayer, He prayed for several things but we will touch on one specifically. Here it is, *"Sanctify them through thy truth: thy word is truth"* (John 17:17). Jesus said *"I am the way the truth and the life."* The simplicity of taking Jesus at His word is awesome. In the book of Revelation, His name is the "Word of God." It seems to be all about Jesus. Yes, dear reader, you are correct. The issue is the Word is a person and so is the Truth. He is praying when He is about to get ripped apart, whipped, spit on, and mocked. He is talking to God about us being sanctified and made holy, while He is soon about to become sin itself. Jesus at this time was soon to become the curse, which was to hang on the tree on our behalf. Here Jesus is talking about sanctification. You hardly ever hear that word in church, and in six years of church, I am not sure I have even heard two sermons on it. As a matter of fact, I haven't! Paul said, *"am I your enemy because I tell you the truth"* (Galatians 4:16). The Truth makes enemies and the cross has enemies. The Truth is the One who went to the cross and became sin so we can be holy. It is Him that is hated. The ultimate lover is hated by men who mind earthly things, whose god is their belly, and whose end is destruction. What is so grand about Jesus, is He loves us so much.

To be hated is not so bad after all, He was and if He lives in us, then we will be too.

The words of the Living God are spirit and life. Jesus has also sent the Spirit of Truth to live in us. His word is truth, His very roo'akh or breath is truth, and truth's color is light. I really believe Jesus wants us to be clean; for this is really a serious thing. Our garments must not be soiled. We can have a real expensive suite, but if it has a stain in it, it becomes worthless. The Truth that sanctifies us, keeps us unspotted from the world. This is huge to Jesus. He prayed it when He was soon to die; it probably was really on His heart. For out of the abundance of the heart the mouth speaks.

We are called to be sanctified wholly in spirit, soul and body. Every area of our lives should be sanctified and consecrated to the Lord Jesus Christ. Our lives should be plumb according to the level of God's Holy Word. The Church should love the Truth, and those who receive not the love of the Truth shall have strong delusion sent by God Himself. *"And with all deceivableness of unrighteousness in them that perish; because they received not the love of the truth, that they might be saved. And for this cause God shall send them strong delusion, that they should believe a lie"* (2 Thessalonians 2:10-11). We can either love the Truth, who God sent, or God Himself will send us a lie. Receive the Truth in the person of His Son; receive the outpouring of the Spirit of Truth, who He sent. Or we can receive strong delusion. Life is full of choices, but this is a no-brainer. We must love the Truth even if it makes us enemies. The Truth will make some enemies and some really good friends. We cannot have the love of God and not love the Truth of God's Word, for love rejoices in truth. Paul really had some good stuff to say. Check this one out; *"But if I tarry long that thou mayest know how thou oughtest to behave thyself in the house of the living God, the pillar and the ground of truth"* (1 Timothy 3:15). Then He goes on to speak of the mystery of godliness, which was the six-fold mystery we briefly touched earlier. Paul speaks about church behavior. If he saw the way young people dress he would fall out of the pew. When people come to church half naked with skintight clothes and see through pants, it is because they are not sanctified and are in need of the Truth. If they are first time visitors they should be loved and welcomed. People who go to church continually should be rebuked for such madness. Church should not be a meat market, but the pillar of Truth. Many leaders do not address it, either because they like it or they are cowards who fear man. Or perhaps their conscience is seared. I don't really know, but Paul would say something. I am a young man, who came out of the world, and the world also came out of me due to truth abiding in my inward parts. I hate to see the world in the church. We are called to go into all the world, not act like the world in hope of them walking in our church one day because we are so much like them. A sanctified person can dress nice, but modestly without a whole lot of flesh hanging out. I have no issue with nice clothes or ripped jeans, but we should be covered. The hearts of men is the ground of truth, for God desires truth in our inward parts. If we are sanctified we will desire what is clean and pure. Unsanctified people love carnal television programs and music that feeds the flesh. Music is either clean or unclean, there is no grey area. It is either Holy Spirit or an unclean spirit. Music either agrees with God's word, or it does not. When we have been sanctified by the word of truth, our desire is to please Jesus and not ourselves. As we become wholly sanctified, Christ's desires begin to wholly posses us. I call that Christianity. Christianity is having Jesus and His desires, and yielding to them wholly. I don't believe in a list of thousands of do's and don'ts. Yet love does have do's and don'ts. (see 1 Corinthians 13)

We are living in a bridal generation. The Lord Jesus' return is at hand, and we are in a season that is two fold. I believe the bride is making herself ready and purity is her highest goal. She is working in the field and compelling the lost to come in before the wedding. She is making her husband known in the city gate, she is not making a name for herself or her ministry, but she is making Him known. This can only happen when the Groom lives in the bride.

The ground of the truth is not a building but a heart; David saw this in a clear way.

Eyes that have been anointed with eye salve from Jesus see Him and what He desires. David, in Psalm 51, sees some of the Lord's desires; what a privilege.

"Behold, thou desirest truth in the inward parts: and in the hidden part thou shall make me to know wisdom" (Psalm 51:6). Desirest means to be pleased and take delight. Jesus delights to live in us and to deliver us from us by having His truth live in us. He takes joy in our freedom. He is happy about it, for He paid a great price for the purchase of the pearl. We are His pearl of great price, He sold everything to purchase us, and we were the joy set before Him. He is crazy about us. If we only knew how much He paid and how much He thinks about us, it would undo us forever.

Freedom comes to those who know the truth. The Truth desires to live in us, and completely free us from us. Jesus said, *"And ye shall know the truth, and the truth shall make you free"* (John 8:32). "It was for freedom Christ set us free." The Holy Spirit's full time job is to keep us free. That is why we are told not to quench Him or grieve Him. Quenching Him and grieving Him only leads to bondage. Jesus came full of grace and grace is for us to stand in. The belt of truth is to keep our pants up while we stand, lest we become naked and ashamed.

Jesus is the way, the truth, and the life. Truth is progressive. Most of the church is filled with facts, not truth. A fact is you have money, the Truth is fervent heat which will consume even the place where you deposit your money. Jesus is the Truth, and He continually reveals Himself in different forms to His disciples. He revealed Himself to John the Revelator in many different ways. A brief example of this is Jesus is Lord, which is true, but then later we find out that Jesus is not just Lord of servants but Lord of Lord's and even King of Kings, who has a name high above any other name. Jesus being Lord is true, but He being Lord of Lord's is a progression of that truth. Seeing this and knowing it must cause us to walk in it; remember Andrew beheld the Lamb and then followed Him.

John the Revelator has a real nugget on this. *"For I rejoiced greatly, when the brethren came and testified of the truth that is in thee, even as thou walkest in the truth. I have no greater joy than to hear that my children walk in truth"* (3 John 1:3-4). Truth is inward, only the inward truth can delight after the law of God. Only Jesus can teach us to love the law because He fulfilled it. He also paid the price for all the lawbreakers to get out of jail free. The internal reality that Jesus' word creates in us is what should determine what and where we walk. We must be led by Truth or we will be lost and deceived. If our belief is not consistent with our experience, our belief is still theory not belief. When we cannot demonstrate what we believe, we are hypocrites. If people are not following us, we may not be a leader. If signs and wonders do not follow us, we may not be believing believers. Jesus said, "these signs follow those who believe." True belief brings about manifestation. Signs and wonders are to follow us; we are not to follow them. The antichrist will have a following because of his signs and wonders, but Jesus' true church still will have signs and wonders following them. The enemy does not persecute what does not threaten him. I believe the two prophets in Revelations 11 are killed because their power is superior to the antichrist spirit's power. Then the Spirit of Life comes in them and raises them from the dead, yet again proving Jesus wins. Those who have truth in the inward parts naturally walk in truth because truth is not hypocritical. Just as Jesus would not ask us to lay down our lives, if He had not already laid down His. Truth leads by example; Truth is heard and seen. The question is, do we have Truth or facts about the Truth? Can we explain sanctification, or are we sanctified? We need to be able to explain what we have, but we really need to have it. If we are in bondage to sin, we cannot have Truth because to know Truth is to be free from sin. The word of God is not bound, neither is the Truth. God has such great plans that just cannot take place from a jail cell. The good news is, that whether we are captives or lawbreakers, He proclaims liberty through the Truth of the Gospel. This is the Good News, we can be free. Many think bad news controls everything and that the television shows are the sign of the times, which is a fact. The truth is the Gospel controls time, not CNN. The Bible says that the "Gospel shall be preached in all the world then the end shall come." This means the Gospel, the good news, is for bad times. We are always supposed to be in the opposite spirit, than the spirit of the age. Everything bad is happening, we are supposed to have good news. The world was starving; Joseph had bread, Babylon needed revelation; and they had to see Daniel. Christians say all kinds of dumb stuff, like I am not called to the lost. What if Jesus was not called to the lost? With a statement like that, you might be lost. Unbelieving believers use every excuse not to do the simple things that Christ anointed us to do. The church has let their disappointment and fears alter their doctrine and manner of life. It is time to return to the Truth and the simplicity of it. Like reading the Bible and doing what it says by praying, fasting, witnessing, healing the sick, and all night prayer and preaching in the day. There comes an hour when no one can work, why not take advantage of freedom while it is still here. When you pray to a real God who hears, preaching comes next. When prayer and prayer meetings are charismatic idols we stay in church, lost in the building with Jesus knocking on the door. Maybe if we go outside we will see Jesus in the sick man or in the hungry man — who knows. What could happen is someone may get saved and sanctified. There are many tithers outside the building, I figure if I say that, maybe someone will go outside. The church needs a vaccination from self that only a cross can give. We need the truth of God's word to pierce us, or there is no hope for them. The world wants truth. They want something solid, something that does not fold when the storms of life blow in. They want the real Jesus that we have yet to show them and offer some living water. Instead, people sell water on television and call it holy; God have mercy on us.

"Looking unto Jesus the author and finisher of our faith; who for the joy set before Him endured the cross, despising the shame, and is set down at the right hand of the throne of God" (Hebrews 12:2).

This verse is marvelous and full of life. It is telling us to look at a Jesus who endured the cross and is risen and seated next to the Father. This sums up the Christian life; a Christian must be well acquainted with the cross on which they have been crucified with Christ. Furthermore, a Christian also should be boldly approaching the throne of grace, which should be daily along with dying to self. Before we do anything, we need our spirit man to hear and see Jesus, or we will be involved in many vain endeavors. The cross is meant for us to carry, and the throne is meant for us to sit on. This is why we need to labor to enter into the rest; what an invitation. The whole thing is so simple; we see Jesus and we then pursue Him. Take up your cross, follow Me; that is pursuing Him. Come boldly to the throne; that is us pursuing Him again. Anything healthy that comes from ministry starts with us pursuing Him or Him pursuing us. The whole point of looking unto Him is so we can come close to Him and be like Him, not so we can have a good journal entry that day or a big ministry. Seeing Jesus with our spirit man will enlarge our heart for sure.

I am very fond of the book of Hebrews. It contains profound statements like these:

"But we see Jesus" (Hebrews 2:9); *"Looking unto Jesus"* (Hebrew 12:2); *"Consider the Apostle and High Priest of our profession Christ Jesus"* (Hebrews 3:1).

Jesus is mentioned so much, it is awesome. Jesus said the "Spirit of the Lord is upon me to preach good news." That is an evangelist's proclamation, for an evangelist preaches good news. We heard some bad news evangelists also, sometimes evangelists who nobody listens to become Jonah-like prophets.

It is very important to meet Jesus on the cross and see Him hanging there for you. There is no throne access unless you meet Jesus on the cross and are washed in His precious blood. Scripture tells us, draw nigh to God and He will draw nigh to you. We are also taught from scripture that the blood of Christ brings us nigh.

(James 4:8 and Ephesians 2:13). If the blood brings us nigh, and it was God's idea for us to have the Bible and the Bible is telling us to draw near, I guess God wants to be real close to us. Only seeing Jesus can help the vast amount of problems we face in this hour. Many of the church's doctrinal differences and divisions are because people do not see Jesus.

I absolutely love the book of Daniel because Jesus appears in so many different ways, He wins my heart over and over as I meditate upon His appearing and wait for His appearance. When He comes every eye will see Him. Some things I noticed in the book of Daniel are that the four young men had no doctrinal differences, no public debates, and no discord among them. They did not fight for position and they were not in competition. The reason being is that they all saw Jesus and were delivered by Him from their adversaries. There was no compromise in any of them; their devotion provoked Jesus to come to their aid. Others saw Jesus, because of their devotion to His word or law. They would not bow their knee to another. Daniel would not stop bowing his knees to the Lord and to the city where His name was written. He was promoted through his uncompromising devotion to the God of Heaven, who came to earth on his behalf. The reality of an authentic relationship with God is it goes both ways, you boldly approach the throne and the One on the throne pursues you. You pray in His name and He prays for you. He speaks to you and you tell the people. It is back and forth. This is what it is like for those who hear and see Jesus, with their inner man. This naturally strengthens our inner man, similar to praying in the Holy Ghost, and it builds up our most holy faith.

Pondering all the different ways Jesus manifested Himself in the scriptures will really help our walk with Christ, and it will be health to our bones. To meditate upon Jesus in the scriptures is the reason the Bible was given to us. Jesus Himself showed them all the things concerning Himself in the scriptures. The scriptures are not to debate, but to make us wise unto salvation as we see the Savior in every page. The scriptures are like Jesus, fully God breathed and fully penned by the hands of men. Jesus was fully God and fully man. Born of a virgin and manifested in the flesh. He is the Passover Lamb, the burnt offering. In the scriptures the verses that Jesus opened were not listed for no reason, it is because He wants to take each child of His on a journey in the holy written Word, to reveal Himself to us. When we begin this journey it is the beginning of a burning heart, which is a lifestyle. He will give us daily bread. It was His idea in the first place, anyway. If our light is going to shine, our heart must burn for the Son of God. A cold heart cannot have light in it, because the light of God's revelation is what causes our hearts to burn. The disciples' hearts burned within them when the scripture was opened and they saw the scriptures from Jesus' view.

We have been given the mind of Christ, so that we can continually live in the place of revelation and we can prove the will of God and please our Father. The disciples saw the scriptures in the light of Jesus' perspective and it caused them to burn. Seeing Jesus is the beginning of this whole thing, and then we see through His eyes. Then we even see others and ourselves through His eyes, hence the mind of Christ. Our natural eyes do not tell us what we are seeing, our brain tells our eyes what our eyes are transmitting. So it is in the spirit, that is why we need the mind of Christ to see the Father's will. Not seeing Jesus will put many in the lake of fire for all of eternity. Seeing Jesus naturally changes those who spiritually see Him. Just ask the two blind men who saw Him with their spirits and cried, "Son of David, have mercy," and He healed them. Jesus did not give them two dollars or a cup of coffee, He opened their blind eyes. That is spiritual mercy, not fleshly compassion that a heathen can have. I believe in feeding and giving a cup of cold water, but I believe signs and wonders follow the believer that is following Jesus. Doesn't the Bible say something like that?

Matthew 25 deals with two kinds of people, those who know Jesus and go out to meet Him, and those who do not know Him and who He tells to depart from Him. Everyone is in one of those categories.

The five foolish virgins all hang out together and man is their source. They try to buy oil from the wise virgins but they won't sell it. No oil in their lamp means no light for their path, they cannot see. This is a huge problem; we see it later very clearly in the same chapter.

"For I was hungry, and ye gave Me no meat: I was thirsty, and ye gave Me no drink: I was a stranger, and ye took Me not in: naked and ye

clothed Me not: sick, and in prison, and ye visited Me not. Then shall they also answer Him, saying, Lord, when saw we Thee hungry, or athirst, or a stranger, or naked, or sick, or in prison, and did not minister unto Thee? Then shall He answer them, saying, Verily I say unto you, inasmuch as ye did it not to one of the least of these, ye did it not to Me. And these shall go away into everlasting punishment: but the righteous into eternal life" (Matthew 25:42-46).

These men and women did not see Jesus in the face of the person in need. Ministry in its purest form is serving those who cannot return the favor. Doing for those who can do nothing for you, this is a Christ centered ministry. We could do nothing for Him, because He died for us while we were yet sinners. He could see the treasure of the pearl through the shell of an oyster, and He was willing to spend Himself for it. As we see Jesus, we will be able to see as He sees. These people could not see Jesus, but these are the people that He mostly ministered to on earth. Did they read their Bible, or were they in it for what Jesus could give them? The humility of Jesus is stunning; the blameless One identifies Himself with a sinner who is in prison. The Jesus who heals us by His stripes identifies Himself with the sick. The very bread of life Himself was hungry, the very Jesus who gives water that will make you never thirst again was thirsty and no one came to Him. The reason being is that they could not see Him. Remember the two blind men saw Jesus through their need. The people who do not see Jesus, do not see Him in the needy person. These people become unaware of their need for Him and stopped serving Him due to the fact that they do not see Him. You cannot serve Jesus if you do not see Him. There is another classic group of people who do not see Jesus. The church of Laodicea, they are so blessed with material goods that they do not see that Jesus is not in their church. The Jesus who was ripped apart on a tree, the

Jesus whose blood was drained out of His body for them, has a real word for them. Remember this is the Jesus that said, "I will never leave you nor forsake you," but He did not say, I will not spit you out of my mouth. In Revelation 3:17, Jesus calls them five names in perfect love. They are poor, naked, miserable, wretched, and blind. This really gets me. How could He say this all in perfect love? So Jesus is name-calling and then He tries to sell them stuff in the very next verse. *"I counsel thee to buy of me gold tried in the fire, that thou mayest be rich; and white raiment, that thou mayest be clothed, and that thy nakedness do not appear; and anoint thine eyes with eye salve, that thou mayest see"* (Revelation 3:18). The fear of God comes on me as I read this, but my heart rejoices as my spirit receives the words of the living God. Jesus is awesome and wonderful; He sells stuff to them who He has purchased with His blood. Jesus is the only one who sells stuff to make you rich. Other salesmen sell things for their gain, yet Jesus desires us to be rich, even after the fact He has already spent every ounce of His blood for you. This pierces my heart to see Jesus make a one time offer for those who want to make a costly offer. When we are poor in spirit we have access to the riches of His grace. Most salesmen sweet-talk you before they try to sell you something, not Jesus! Jesus' ways are breathtaking. Jesus takes my breath away and causes my eyes to leak frequently. Eyes that do not usually leak need eye salve more frequently than eyes that do leak. Jesus has a solution for their entire problem, but it is not free. It will cost everything to the buyer. Are we willing? The eyes that need to be anointed, and the lamp that needs oil. Jesus has and is everything we need. Jesus did not sell anything in His earthly ministry, but He desires that we buy gold tried in the fire. For someone to make a purchase from someone they cannot see, takes faith. If we cannot see Jesus in the needy person in front of us, we are certainly not ready for His return. In that aspect, the last thing that we would want to hear about is a Jesus on a white horse who comes to make war on the earth. The Jesus who comes on a white horse, comes to take vengeance on everything that hinders love. There will be no variables when He returns and no one can stop Him. No prayer meeting will keep Him from fulfilling His word. No ecumenical picture of what men depict Jesus to be will be able to stand the fervent heat of His coming. The great and the terrible day draws near, we must hear Jesus today. The church of Laodicea did not recognize that Jesus was not there. Their abundance blinded them to the only thing worth seeing, Jesus. See the humility and the kindness of Jesus when He knocks on the door, still desiring to come in and eat with them after they forgot all about Him. The point of the scripture is not to bash Laodicea, but to show the humility and greatness of Jesus and how He pursues even those who have forgot about Him. It illustrates how He wants us to be rich through our purchase from Him. The fact is that He wants to eat with us and desires us to sit with Him in His throne. We are invited to approach boldly. Think of the privilege His blood has bought us, He tells us to boldly approach, yet He humbly knocks on our door. He is so good, and He wants us to taste and see. Then we will naturally tell others so that His house may be full. If we taste, we will see...

"He that hath an ear, let him hear what the Spirit saith unto the churches" (Revelation 3:22).

We live by what proceeds, not by what has proceeded. That is why we need our daily bread. When we have ears to hear what the Spirit is saying, it is so that we can live by and from what we are hearing. Jesus understood this very well, because this Truth is rooted in Him who is the Truth. Every time Jesus finished His discourse to the seven churches in the book of Revelation He said, *"He that has ears to hear, let him hear what the Spirit says to the church."* Faith does not come by having heard, but by continually hearing. We must be present with God in the moment or we could seriously miss what God wants to say and do.

Isaac definitely understands that we live by every word that proceeds from the mouth of God. If Abraham would not have heard the angel of the Lord from heaven speaking God's right-now word, he would have been dead. We really do live by every word that proceeds from the mouth of God, just ask Isaac when you get to heaven. I could just imagine Isaac as part of the great cloud of witnesses smirking at his father Abraham when Jesus said to Satan, "man lives by every word that proceeds from the mouth of God." *"But he answered and said, It is written, man shall not live by bread alone, but by every word that proceedeth out of the mouth of God"* (Matthew 4:4). When we have ears to hear what the Spirit is saying, it is so that we can live by and from what we are hearing. When we truly fear God, our primary desire is to hear and obey Him. This is how we show God we love Him. In the obedience of faith that comes from hearing the Word of God, the world can see our love for Jesus. Jesus illustrated or modeled radical love for the Father by obeying Him and hearing Him even when He was silent.

"For the life of the flesh is in the blood: and I have given it to you upon the altar to make an atonement for your soul: for it is the blood that maketh an atonement for the soul" (Leviticus 17:11). This verse shows us several things. One of them being that we clearly know abortion is murder, because the baby that the savage money hungry doctors call a "fetus" is clearly a living person because of the blood in it's precious little veins. In this, we clearly learn that "life is in the blood." So with this understanding, let us fast forward a few thousand years and go directly to Jesus in the Garden of Gethsemane. Here we find Jesus praying. It is typical that the church is sleeping and Jesus is praying.

"And He was withdrawn from them about a stone's cast, and kneeled down, and prayed, saying, Father if thou be willing, remove this cup from Me: nevertheless not My will, but Thine, be done. And there appeared an angel unto Him from heaven, strengthening Him. And being in agony He prayed the more earnestly: and His sweat was as it were great drops of blood falling to the ground. And when He rose up from prayer, and was come to His disciples, He found them sleeping for sorrow" (Luke 22:41-45). Jesus is praying and the Father is not speaking. The Father responds, but not with words. Jesus lived by every word that proceeded from the mouth of God. Therefore, when God His Father stopped speaking, He started bleeding, because life is in the blood and His blood was leaking out of Him because the Father stopped speaking to Him. The Father sent the angel to strengthen Him so He could lay down His life. When Jeremiah said, *"see the Word of the Lord,"* I think he was talking about Jesus. The beauty of scripture is we get to see Jesus. As we read God's

word and He opens the eyes of our understanding, we begin to see this great invitation we have in Christ Jesus. We begin to discover the unsearchable riches of Christ as His word begins to dwell in us richly. Christ shares His unsearchable riches with us, by allowing His word to dwell in us richly in all wisdom. In the Proverbs we learn that natural riches are not comparable to wisdom. Spiritual wealth comes from God's word and is applied to our lives by God's Holy Spirit who lives inside of us. As the word of God is spoken, the Spirit of God then begins to move.

Before the Spirit of the Lord came upon David, God first spoke to Samuel and instructed him who he was to anoint. God choosing David was contrary to Samuel's opinion that was shaped similar to our opinion by what we see. God's word often is contrary to the flesh, both God's word and His Spirit are contrary to the flesh and the control the flesh loves. If we are living by what God is truly saying, we will not be in control, He will. Jesus is really only our Lord when we do what He has said in His Word and is saying by His Spirit. In our obedience to what Jesus is saying, He becomes visible to others around us; this is called ministry. Samuel anointed David at the word of the Lord. Then David in Psalm 23 said, "you anoint my head with oil." As I was reading this, the Lord spoke to me and said "Adam, I never anointed David's head, Samuel did. Yet when he obeyed My word, he became invisible and David saw Me." The obedience of faith puts Jesus on display, which is what ministry is. Ministry is not just serving God, but presenting Him for who He really is. So many people have misrepresented Jesus. Hearing God and obeying allows us to re-present Him for who He really is. This makes us part of the solution, and that is good news.

"I will worship toward thy holy temple, and praise thy name for thy loving kindness and for thy truth: for thou hast magnified thy word above all thy name" (Psalm 138:2).

As I was reading this verse one day I stopped and said, Lord I really don't get this. How do you exalt your word above your own name? He said, "simple, with My word I created all things. By My word I hold all things together. In the world I created, I came and gave My life according to the word I spoke through the mouth of My prophets. When for three days you could not call upon My name, My word held My dead body and the planet where I commanded it to be. Even while I was dead, My word was alive. According to My word, by the Spirit of Holiness, I rose Myself from the dead. Hence I have the power to lay My life down and take it up again; all this is my Father's glory."

When the Lord spoke to me, this just broke my heart. I began to weep, overwhelmed with the greatness of Jesus and His kindness to immediately answer me on such a profound topic. In the gospel of John Jesus said, "The Father loves the Son and shows Him all things." It was the Father's affections that allowed Jesus to respond to me by His Holy Spirit; this is overwhelming to anyone with a heartbeat. If you spend time in God's word you will become deeply fascinated with the Son of God. One of the ways God communicates love to His children is by revelation, hence "The Father loves the Son, and shows Him all things." The voice of God is to bring forth a revelation of Jesus Christ. When Jesus was baptized at the river Jordan, the audible voice of God and the outpouring of the Holy Spirit were both focused directly on Christ Jesus. The study of the scriptures, the Father's voice and the outpouring of the Spirit are all centered on Christ Jesus. God's voice and the power of the Holy Spirit are to bring forth a revelation of Christ Jesus. **My prayer for you is that you would know and feel the Father's love for His Son Jesus and the way Jesus knew the Father's love, you would know it and abide in it and give it away to a dying world.**

weseejesus
MINISTRIES

Adam LiVecchi, the leader of We See Jesus Ministries, lives by faith and has a heart to bring the Word of the Lord to the Body of Christ. His ministry is an itinerant ministry based in Northern NJ. As a result of the Lord's leading he has had the opportunity to minister internationally in Honduras, China, Mexico, Philippines, India, Peru, Dominican Republic, Brazil, Nicaragua, Haiti, Canada, Uruguay and all across the United States.

We See Jesus Ministries seeks to build the Kingdom of God through equipping the local church and delivering the Gospel message with signs and wonders following. Adam has the privilege of traveling with his beautiful wife, Sarah, and his brother, Aaron, who are both anointed musicians. Adam is also the co-leader of Voices in the Wilderness School of the Prophets rooted out of his local church in Woodland Park, NJ. Adam and Sarah LiVecchi look forward to building long lasting relationships that lead to sustainable change for the glory of King Jesus.

We See Jesus Ministries
31 Werneking Place
Little Ferry, NJ 07643
(973) 296-9050
WeSeeJesusMinistries.com
info@weseejesusministries.com

Voices in the Wilderness
School of the Prophets
86 Lackawana Ave
Suite 243
Woodland Park, NJ 07424
VoicesintheWilderness.us
info@voicesinthewilderness.us